AWAY TO ME, MOSS

BETTY LEVIN

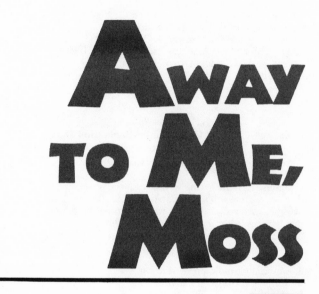

AWAY TO ME, MOSS

Greenwillow Books
New York

Library of Congress Cataloging-in-Publication Data
Levin, Betty.
  Away to me, Moss / by Betty Levin.
      p.   cm.
  Summary: While trying to deal with the possibility
that her parents will separate, ten-year-old Zanna
becomes involved in working with a spirited sheepdog
that belongs to the stroke patient her mother is
helping to rehabilitate.
  ISBN 0-688-13439-4
  [1. Sheep dogs—Fiction.   2. Dogs—Fiction.
3. Physically handicapped—Fiction.
4. Family problems—Fiction.]
I. Title.   PZ7.L5759Aw   1994
[Fic]—dc20
93-48136   CIP   AC

To those in the coming generation who understand
the working partnership between dogs and people:

Mina and Foster Bartovics
Caitlin and Nora Burke
Jay Canaday
Colin Kennard
Debbie Merrill
Dave Murray
Heather Murray
Karin Peterson
Erich and Stacy Pobatschnig
Graham Webster
Simon White

Some of you have already braved the trials;
others simply help from time to time in barns and fields.
Yet all of you carry forward the herding tradition.

CONTENTS

PART ONE   1

PART TWO   41

PART THREE   95

PART FOUR   121

GLOSSARY   159

AWAY TO ME, MOSS

1 Zanna Wald and her sister, Rachel, sprawled on the cold concrete floor of the old cow barn with puppies tumbling all over them. Laurie Catherwood, who could play with the puppies any old time, stood waiting for Rachel to pick out her favorite.

Zanna thought they looked pretty much alike. Each one was mostly black with white on the face and chest and around the neck. The feet and tail tips were white, too.

Rachel was looking for the one with the most even white markings.

"This one!" she announced as she swept up a puppy and held it aloft. Its white-tipped tail beat the air like a stubby pendulum. Its pink tongue lapped at her.

"That one's a girl," Laurie told her. "All the girls are spoken for."

Rachel set the puppy down. "I bet all the best ones are," she returned. "All the classy-looking ones."

Laurie said, "It's a good thing Grampa can't hear you. He says with Border Collies it's what they do, not what they look like, that counts."

Rachel pulled another puppy out of the heap. But when she saw that the white blaze on its face was dotted with black, she set it aside. Zanna understood that Rachel would never settle for anything that was less than perfect.

Without realizing it, Zanna raised her hand to her own face, as if to cover the freckles on and around her nose.

"So when will you talk to your mother?" Laurie asked Rachel.

"When she's in a better mood. Can't you get your parents to save one for me?"

"I did sort of mention it," Laurie said. "The thing is, they don't think they can charge your mom full price."

Rachel ducked her head. One of the puppies leaped clumsily, grabbed a mouthful of hair, and began to tug. "Ow!" Rachel cried. She pried open the tiny jaws and then stood up. "I'll ask my dad the next time he calls. Tell your parents I'll get the money, all of it."

Laurie said, "Someone's coming today to look at the pups, someone that wants to see Meg and Moss work sheep, since they're the puppies' parents. Dad hates showing Moss to people." She glanced toward the end of the barn where a mostly black Border Collie lay chained to a ring in the wall.

"I don't blame him," Rachel responded. "Moss always looks so dirty."

Zanna gazed at Moss. As far as she could tell, he was always there like that. Just lying at the end of the chain. Something drew her toward him. The closer she came, the stranger she felt. She was used to Meg's prancing, joyful greeting, but with Moss she met utter disregard.

Crouching down, she spoke his name. His dark eyes shifted slightly. He certainly wasn't classy-looking. It didn't help knowing that the black spots on his white muzzle were natural markings. He did look dirty lying there with his chin on his mottled forepaws, not moving.

Just then Meg leaped the barrier at the other end of the cow barn and ran to her puppies. They swarmed around her, trying to nurse, but she stood for only a moment before wheeling away and soaring over the barrier again.

Moss had risen at Meg's entrance. Now he dropped to the floor again.

"Does Moss ever get out like Meg?" Zanna asked Laurie.

Laurie nodded. "First thing every morning. Before they get Grampa up. But they can't leave Moss loose for long, or he'll get in trouble. He's always sneaking after the heifers or jumping the gate to work the sheep. And when Grampa's out in the wheel-chair, Moss won't let him alone. So mostly he's chained up."

"Don't they like him?" Zanna pursued.

"Like?" Laurie was stumped by that question.

"Well, why keep him if he's just tied up all day?"

"I don't know," Laurie answered. "He's—he was Grampa's special dog. Grampa thought he had the makings of a champion. He was just beginning to run him in open trials before he had the stroke."

Zanna didn't say anything more. Later she might ask her mother about Laurie's grandfather. Mom was Rob Catherwood's speech therapist. She also gave him physical therapy twice a day to help him recover some use of his right side, which was mostly paralyzed. Mom would know whether there was any hope for Rob to get back to working his dog again.

"Zanna!" Rachel called from the far side of the barrier. "Time to go home. We've got to figure out how to get the puppy."

The dog on the chain had eyes so dark they glinted almost green in the dimness of the barn. Zanna extended her hand. She could feel the warm breath on her fingertips. How could anything alive be so still? She spoke his name again: "Moss." Then she rose and waded out through the clamorous puppies.

Rachel was waiting for her in the barnyard, which was crammed with farm machinery. Zanna had learned to keep clear of the bad-tempered hen that nested beneath the rusted metal parts.

On the way home Rachel tried to get Zanna to figure out a plan for wheedling a puppy out of their mother. Rachel was counting on Zanna to promise to clean up after the puppy in the afternoons since she was always the first one home from school.

"But I thought you wanted a kitten," Zanna reminded her.

"I did. That was before these puppies got to be so cute."

As soon as Zanna tried to imagine having one, she found herself thinking about Moss instead. She wished she had touched him. She wished she had found a way to let him know that he wasn't entirely forgotten.

2

Rachel's plan was to get up early on Saturday and go with Mom to the farm. After Rob Catherwood's therapy Rachel would be ready with the puppies. Mom was bound to see how adorable and irresistible they were.

But the plan fell through when Dad decided to detour east on his way to a conference he had to attend for his work. He would snatch the weekend home with his family.

Zanna was so elated she forgot all about the puppy. But Rachel didn't. "It's fate," she declared. "Dad's just what we need."

Zanna agreed that they needed Dad, but that wasn't what Rachel meant.

It was Zanna who had spent so much time with Dad when they first moved onto Ragged Mountain. He was still out of work then and had almost always been home when the school bus dropped her off. She would join him in some project around the place or over at the farm. "The good life," he called it as they picked apples and put up jars and jars of applesauce. "This is the way to live," he declared as they fixed up the old chicken coop to house the exotic fowl people were giving away at the end of the fair season.

Mom had been skeptical about this project. The hens were up for grabs because they wouldn't be laying much more. Dad said it would cost practically nothing if they were allowed to forage for seeds and bugs. The trouble was that raccoons and foxes foraged, too. One after another, the fowl had vanished. Zanna and Dad would come across a severed head or just a heap of feathers.

"And not one egg," Mom had commented. "Ever."

"Never mind," Dad had replied. "It's nature's way. And the effort wasn't wasted. Zanna learned how to use a drill without getting the bit stuck. We can start again in the spring with more precautions."

Now it was coming on to spring, but Dad was way off in California. If things worked out, the company where he was consulting would probably take him on full-time, and then they would all move again. Meanwhile, Mom and Zanna and Rachel lived up here on Ragged Mountain in Laurie's house, since Laurie and her family had moved into the big farmhouse to help take care of Laurie's grandfather and to be on hand for all those chores he could no longer do.

Dad would be home for the first time since Christmas. Because he was arriving while Mom was at work, he planned to rent a car at the airport. Zanna imagined him waiting for her Friday after school.

On that day she ran all the way to the curve in the driveway. No car. She stopped, breathless and aching with disappointment. Maybe he had driven over to the farm.

Zanna turned and headed for the Catherwoods'. Soon the new farm buildings below the road came into view, the cows grouped outside the pole barn. In another hour or so they would move closer to the milking parlor.

Looking uphill to her left, Zanna caught sight of a shiny car in the Catherwood driveway. It had to be Dad's rented one. To avoid the muddy ruts, she detoured onto the lawn. But that brought her into Rob Catherwood's line of vision. He sat, all bundled up, on the porch so that he could look out to the lower farm and the steep slope down the mountain. Fennella, Laurie's grandmother, said that he liked being outdoors, even when it was nippy, because it made him feel less trapped.

Zanna slowed and approached the man in the wheelchair. Now that he had seen her, she knew she had to speak to him. It felt weird to call him Rob, but there were so many Catherwoods here that she was supposed to use each one's first name. Rob and Fennella were the oldest. Then came Gordon, who was their son, and Dot, who was Gordon's wife. They were Laurie's and Dave's parents, and also Janet's. Janet was married, but she lived nearby.

"Hi, Rob," Zanna said. "I've come looking for my dad." Would it be all right to leave now? She was supposed to look Rob in the eye, but she was afraid she might end up staring at his mouth, which sagged and sometimes drooled.

She knew that he could nod and even speak a word or two when he felt like it. There was nothing wrong with his understanding. All the same, it was hard to carry on a one-sided conversation with him. Once she had seen him swing his left knee a bit, but his left arm had been so badly shattered that it was still useless. No one knew for sure whether the stroke had come first or whether his fall from the barn roof had triggered the stroke.

She was just starting to back away from the porch when she heard an angry shout. She froze. "That'll do, Moss," Gordon roared. Zanna didn't want to go near that temper, not even to find her father.

Moss came bounding around to the front of the house. He cut in front of Zanna, scrambled up the steps, and hurled himself at Rob. The wheelchair veered sideways. Zanna ran up to the porch, reached for the dog's collar, and yanked at him, pulling the blanket down with Moss. She didn't know what to do next, so she just clung to the dog.

Fennella, who always seemed to move in quick darts, came banging out of the house. Except for the stoop in her shoulders, she had a spare look that made her seem not much older than

Dot, her daughter-in-law. Deftly she snapped up the blanket, shook it out, and wrapped it around Rob. "That dog," she scolded. "If he's not the death of you, he'll drive Gordon crazy." Picking up Rob's right arm and folding it across his lap, she explained to Zanna that when Moss nudged Rob's arm off the chair, it all but dislocated Rob's shoulder.

Gordon came storming after Moss. "I was trying to show Howard Nearing the dogs. He may buy one of the pups."

Rob uttered a strangled sound and then spit out one word: "God!"

"Howard Nearing?" Fennella declared. "Rob can't stand the man."

"Well," Gordon retorted, "we can stand his money. Of course, he wanted to see Meg and Moss work. Meg was looking good, but Moss charged after the sheep. Then he took off like he does. So Howard Nearing said forget it, he'd come back some other time."

Even as Gordon spoke, the shiny car headed out the driveway. They all watched it go. Then Gordon turned to Rob. "I'm sorry, Dad," he said. "I know how you feel about the dog. But we just don't get along." The anger was gone from his voice. Now he was Laurie's approachable father, overworked but not unkind.

Zanna felt easy enough to tell him she had thought the shiny car was Dad's rental one. Gordon said he wished it had been, and Fennella suggested that Zanna go play with the puppies. That would make the time go faster, and her dad would be here before she knew it.

"Could I take Moss for a walk instead?" Zanna heard herself asking.

A quick glance passed between Fennella and Gordon. Then Gordon said to wait until he fetched some baler twine, so that Moss couldn't run out on her.

Zanna had imagined racing through a field with Moss free at

her side. But she was willing to take him on any terms, just so long as he didn't have to be dragged away from Rob to be chained up at the back of the barn just yet.

3 The walk with Moss was more like a sprint. First he dragged Zanna toward the gate to the sheep pasture. She hauled back on the twine; it cut into her palm. Finally she grabbed his collar and headed him around behind the barn. When she tried holding the twine again, Moss was more responsive to her tugs. Still, it was a struggle getting him through the field of winter rye. Either he hung back or he hurtled forward. There was no walking.

Once they reached the woodlot, though, Moss calmed down. Here were scents to lure him or to stop him in his tracks. She tried to keep up without choking him, all the time saying his name. When he rushed at a squirrel, she named that, too, and afterward the hollow log where Moss sniffed at each end. "Maybe a raccoon," she told him. That made her think of Dad's hens that had been food for the raccoon or the fox or the weasel. Or all three. And that made her think of Dad, who might be driving up to an empty house at this very moment.

"We have to go back," she said to Moss. His head swiveled. But his alertness had nothing to do with her. He was intent on something in the distance. "Next time," she promised as she forced him to turn uphill toward the barn, "you'll stay out longer. You'll have a real run."

In the barn Moss scrambled to get away from the puppies. The moment Zanna hitched him, he sank down, dropping his muzzle to the floor.

Zanna headed home through the pasture shortcut. There were Rachel and Dad. And the car, not as shiny as Howard Nearing's, but a lot newer than Mom's. She threw herself at Dad, who wrapped his arms around her and held her hard.

"How long can you stay?" Zanna wanted to know. She needed to steel herself against his leaving.

The girls helped him finish unloading the car. He had shopped at the big supermarket across from the airport. He intended to cook up a storm, he said. It felt good to be in a real kitchen again, good to see his daughters, good to look forward to a weekend with his family.

When he went upstairs to change, Rachel told Zanna that she had already spoken to him about the puppy and he'd said it sounded like a great idea. "He promised to speak to Mom," Rachel added.

The girls set to work washing and slicing vegetables for the great pasta sauce Dad wanted to make. He asked them all about school and friends. He was so eager to hear everything that sometimes he just kept on asking right through their answers. He had bought a lot of fancy ingredients for his sauce. Zanna didn't know what most of them were.

"Don't you ever cook in California?" she asked.

"Not much. Where I'm staying, the kitchen's just a corner of the room. It's called a studio."

Zanna thought of a movie studio. She tried to picture the California she knew through television. All she could see were Hollywood mansions and stores with real live models. It wouldn't be anything like where they had lived in town last year after Dad had lost his job and they had been forced to sell their house in Prescott Falls. Dad had borrowed a lot of money to invest in a property that would be developed into vacation homes and make them rich. Only something had gone wrong that wasn't anyone's fault. It was the timing, Dad had explained. The bottom had dropped out of the real estate market. Mom's work at the hospital and Dad's part-time jobs had made it possible to rent the small house in Coventry, which Rachel had loved, because they were close to everything and everyone.

It was Zanna who had been thrilled when they left town to move onto Ragged Mountain. Mom was relieved because it would help them get out of debt. Dad was excited because it felt like a fresh start. Only Rachel had grumbled and resisted. That was before she met Dave Catherwood and discovered that if she signed up for a lot of after-school activities, she got to come home with him on the bus from the high school.

"If we all go to California," Zanna asked, "will we have our own furniture again?"

"Of course. Eventually. Mom may not want to move lock, stock, and barrel until she's sure—"

"—that she's not giving up her own job for nothing," Mom finished for him.

Dad swung around to hug her. Looking over his shoulder, she took in the array of exotic foods and began to shake her head. Dad guessed what she was shaking at and tried to coax her into approval. This was a celebration dinner, he insisted. She relented finally, but she looked drawn and wary.

Zanna could almost feel Mom's fatigue. She knew that if Dad weren't here, Mom would probably go upstairs and flop on the bed for a while before gathering the energy to go to the Catherwoods' to work with Rob. She wished Dad would notice, too, and suggest that Mom rest before supper. But he was so full of the moment among them that he never thought of sending Mom off, even for half an hour. They were going to have fun together. They were going to have one great weekend. It was starting right now.

4 The first argument was about whether to take care of Rob before or after supper. The girls backed off. They could hear Mom's voice go flat as she told Dad that she needed to get the job done while she was still on her feet. Dad gave in. Sounding apologetic, he said he would turn off the heat under his sauce and walk with her to the Catherwoods'.

As soon as Mom and Dad were out the door, Rachel suggested that she and Zanna clean up the kitchen and get the table set. That would show Mom how well they could cope with the mess a puppy would make. But once everything was ready for supper, Rachel began to worry about whether she was missing her best chance to show Dad the pups and win Mom over. She tried to talk Zanna into going over to the farm with her, but Zanna held back. So Rachel, who couldn't stand doing nothing, went along by herself.

Zanna walked through the living room to the closed-in porch where all their furniture was stored. She opened the door and looked onto the strange landscape of peaks and planes and angles beneath sheets and bedspreads. It smelled like home, like Dad and Mom and their old house in Prescott Falls and Sparky the dog, who was killed by a car when they moved into town, and Renee the cat, who disappeared when they moved up here to Ragged Mountain.

Zanna had made a nest on her old bed, which stood high up on top of Rachel's bed. A bureau at one end formed a wall; a small table at the other end fenced in the nest. Zanna had retrieved some of her outgrown things from a packing box, her Eeyore donkey and some other stuffed animals. She was too old to play with them anymore, but she liked to have them with her when she climbed up onto the bed to read or just to think.

When Mom and Dad returned, she could hear them arguing before they actually entered the house. Well, not exactly arguing.

"I didn't think," Dad was saying. "I was just so glad to see her."

"So you thought you could come home and be Santa Claus and then go away again, leaving me with the consequences?"

"You're right, Claire. I wanted to make her happy."

Zanna scrambled off the bed. She had to be out of the furniture room before her parents came through the front door, so they wouldn't think she had been eavesdropping. She nearly knocked over a floor lamp on her way to the hall, but she made it.

"Everything's ready," she said. "Me and Rachel set the big table."

"Rachel and I," Mom corrected, adding as an afterthought, "Thank you."

"How about some wine?" Dad called to Mom. He was already in the kitchen to reheat the sauce and start the water boiling.

"We don't have any," Mom replied. She turned to Zanna. "I suppose you're in on this puppy thing, too?"

Zanna nodded. "Sort of."

"Well, I'm afraid it's out of the question. I'm not surprised that you want one. But Rachel? She wasn't even very attached to Sparky."

"It's her new interest," Zanna explained.

Mom shook her head. "Your father will have to deal with her. I'm too beat."

Dad came in with two glasses of wine. "I didn't come home empty-handed," he declared as he gave Mom hers.

"Santa Claus," she murmured. Dad turned away for a moment. Then he rallied, suggesting they drink to better times ahead.

"Why not?" Mom said. "I'll drink to them, but I won't hold my breath."

Dad began to tell her about his work. The company, still

struggling to get itself established, was building a new lab. Mom asked why they didn't hire him full-time before spending money on a lab. He was just starting to explain about requirements for government approval when Rachel came in and slammed the door behind her. Dad broke off. Mom nodded meaningfully in Rachel's direction.

"Rachel," Dad called. "Sweetheart, will you come into the living room for a minute?"

Rachel stopped at the entrance from the front hall and gazed stonily at the floor.

"We're about to have supper," Dad said to her. "Let's clear the air so that we can enjoy being together."

Rachel's head swung up. "You said it was a terrific idea, just what we needed. How could you go back on that?"

"Because I was wrong. Sweetheart, listen to me. It was a terrific idea. As soon as we're all settled again, I promise you a puppy, any kind you want. It's just not workable now."

"I don't want any kind. I want one of those." A tear dribbled down Rachel's cheek.

"Sweetheart, I know." Dad spread out his arms, and she let him enfold her.

"It isn't fair," she declared, her voice muffled. "Mom made you say this."

Zanna glanced over at Mom, who was holding her glass of wine in front of her and staring through the ruby liquid at the waning light.

"I'm saying it because it's true," Dad told Rachel. "Sometimes second thoughts change first reactions. No one's home all day. Besides, there's the cost, and—"

"I'd earn the money. I can sell my bike. I'll pay you back."

Sighing, Mom turned to Dad and Rachel. "Even if we didn't have to pay the full price, there's so much more, like vet bills. But the main thing is we can't do this to the Catherwoods.

They're desperate for money. Every sale counts. Besides, Rob thinks all Border Collies are meant to be working dogs, not pets."

"That's right," Dad chimed in. "We have to think of Rob. Dot was saying how much progress he's making. They're all amazed at what you're getting him to do."

"There is some progress," Mom responded almost grudgingly. But she looked pleased. They were off on an easier subject now, Rob's condition. Dad released Rachel, who stared at the floor again.

"Thanks for nothing," she muttered under her breath.

Only Zanna heard her.

5 At supper that night Mom and Dad kept the conversation moving from one neutral subject to another. Dad's stepmother in New Jersey was going to have an operation on her hip. Mom's brother was getting married. Again. Old friends whose kids were all in their teens were having another baby. Mom's car was acting up. Again. The porch steps were rotting out.

"I'll try to do something about them while I'm home," Dad said. "If Gordon has any decent scrap lumber."

Rachel signaled Zanna with her eyes. As soon as the girls had cleared the table, she drew Zanna aside. "We have to help," Rachel declared "They might still change their minds about the puppy."

"Help with what?" Zanna asked.

"Help Dad with the porch steps. Help Mom with . . . whatever she does on weekends. Laundry. Shopping. Stuff like that."

Zanna hated shopping. "I'll work with Dad."

Rachel nodded. "And when you're with him at the farm, make sure he sees you playing with the puppies."

Zanna didn't bother to tell Rachel that their parents sounded pretty final about a puppy. Anyway, she was thinking about Moss now. She could see him in her mind's eye, just as he probably was at this very moment, his dark, intense eyes wide and watchful, his body slumped as if resigned to confinement. Tomorrow she would speak to him again. She would try to lift his speckled muzzle from its sunken perch on his forepaws.

But on Saturday morning Moss wasn't in the cow barn. While Rachel and Laurie carried the puppies out into the sunshine, Zanna went with Dad, who found Gordon working Meg for prospective puppy customers. Moss was there, too, tied to the gate.

While Meg brought the yearling flock straight to Gordon, he spoke to the couple who were watching. "I use Meg mostly with the cows," he said. "My father used to trial her." He told Meg to go and drive them away. She was quick and eager, but she paced herself so that the sheep moved smoothly, neither dawdling nor hurried. She carried herself with true Border Collie style, head and tail low, all her intelligence and energy focused on the task. At Gordon's command, she turned the sheep and drove them at an angle. It was a lovely sight, and everyone, including Moss, watched with rapt attention. When Gordon called her back, she came at once and dropped to the ground, still tense, awaiting the next command.

But Gordon told her to stay. He unhitched Moss. "This one doesn't mind too good," Gordon explained to the couple. "I guess he's a one-man dog. My father's." Even as he spoke, Moss took off. At a dead run. "Moss!" Gordon roared. "Lie down!"

But Moss was deaf to Gordon's words. The sheep charged down the field as if the devil were after them, Moss closing the gap between them.

"Moss, get back out!" Gordon ordered. The sheep swerved. Moss held them with his intense gaze.

The couple exchanged glances. Dad stepped in and tried to speak up for Gordon, who was dealing with Moss. Dad said that Rob Catherwood had been training this dog at the time he had his stroke. Moss hadn't been worked properly in over six months.

The man said, "Still, you can't help wonder whether that stubbornness is passed on to the offspring."

Gordon had Moss driving the sheep now, but it was clear that the dog had them all on edge. When Gordon told him, "That'll do," Moss ignored this order to leave the sheep. Gordon had to yell at him to make him obey.

"He's a lot of dog," Gordon admitted as he hitched Moss to the gate. "But you'd never have guessed it when my father was working him."

The man nodded. "I don't think we're up to anything that hard, though. We like the mother dog. Nice and handy, easygoing." As he spoke, the woman stooped to pat Meg, who squirmed with joy.

Zanna dropped to her knees beside Moss. When she placed her hand on his white ruff, he turned for an instant, his moist nose making abrupt contact with her lowered face before he turned back to fix his gaze on the sheep, spread out now and grazing on last year's dead grass.

"Moss," she murmured. "Good boy, Moss."

She looked up and around. Gordon and Dad were going off in one direction, Meg freely following. The couple, on their way to the car, paused to look at the puppies frolicking on the lawn.

Zanna got up and raced to catch up with Gordon and Dad. "Could I put Moss away for you?" she asked Gordon. In a way that would be helping Dad because Gordon always had too much to do and Dad needed to get some lumber from him. "Could I maybe take him for a walk, too?"

When Gordon nodded, Zanna ran back to Moss. Freeing his

rope from the gate, she gave him a tug. He sat up like an old dog that is too stiff to move much. He was still intent on the grazing sheep. "Come!" she urged, yanking harder. He allowed her to lead him away, but he walked as though he had his brakes on. His tail clung to his hindquarters; his ears drooped. "Moss, Moss," she kept saying to him as she dragged him onto the road and turned left.

Below her, to the right, sprawled the new buildings of the lower farm. Next came open fields. She led Moss through a barway onto bleached yellow stubble crusted here and there with frozen snow. When she tried to coax Moss to run with her, the most she could get out of him was a grudging trot. She thought of his speed and power when he gathered the sheep. Maybe the rope held him back. She looked around. They were a good distance from the road now. There was only this expanse of frost-struck grass. It looked perfectly safe.

Zanna dropped her end of the rope and tore across the tawny field, calling Moss. He started to lope along after her. As he moved, his body changed, his head raised and searching. She was so caught up with him that she never noticed the woodchuck hole ahead of her. One wrong step was all it took for her ankle to be painfully wrenched. Down she went, with the wind knocked out of her.

Moss kept right on running. For a moment she simply clutched her leg and rocked. But she tried to keep an eye on the dog. He was circling now, cutting a wide swath far from her, his head down, on the scent of something that curved in and out along the deepening slope.

Recovering her breath, she summoned him with all the authority she could muster. He kept on running. What if she couldn't call him back? What if he disappeared?

She rubbed her ankle, wiggled it a little, and got to her feet.

The ground had sent a chill through her. She couldn't stop shivering. All she could think of was how tired Moss must be of being tied in the barn. Why should he answer her call? He hardly knew her.

She started running again. Her ankle hurt. Her knees rubbed inside her muddy jeans. One moment she was calling and lurching after him, and the next she was sobbing. What was the point of trying to catch him when he could outrun her? What was the point of calling when he could be as stubborn and deaf as he had been with Gordon?

She dropped to the ground. What would Mom say when she found out that Zanna had lost Rob's special dog? What would Rachel say when Zanna had proved that she was irresponsible and unworthy of caring for any dog, let alone a helpless puppy? And what would Moss do on his own? Would he starve? What if Moss came back secretly at night and killed a sheep? Zanna had seen TV movies like that, where a dog went wild and turned savage and had to be shot. Thinking of his being hunted down made her cry even harder.

When Moss thrust his blotchy white and black muzzle into her face, she was so surprised she didn't think to grab his rope. Instead she flung her arms around his head and hauled him up against her. He submitted for only a moment before pulling away, once again aloof and wary. Rising to her knees, she lunged at him. His backward leap was an instinctive reaction. Puzzled and resistant, he stood off from her.

She rubbed the ground between them, separating a clump of dead grass. "Moss," she said, not looking at him, "here. Come here." She flattened the grass and then let it go, leaving her hands open on either side of it. Slowly the grass straightened. He came and sank down between her hands, his nose at the edge of the clump, as if he, too, were watching the separate blades rise up.

Taking the end of the rope, she told him how good he was. She promised to be his friend, and he let her stroke his head and ears without straining away from her, without even looking uncomfortable.

She waited until she could no longer bear the cold that came up from the ground. She waited in the hope that he wouldn't feel himself tricked or betrayed. Then she got up and walked him home.

6 It seemed to Zanna as though she had been away for hours. Yet now, returning, it was as if she had been gone for only an instant. Rachel and Laurie were still on the lawn, the puppies spread out around them. Rob was not yet on the porch. Could Mom still be inside giving him his therapy? No one, not anyone in the entire world, had any inkling of where Zanna had been or of what had happened. And not happened.

Moss walked beside her, neither straining nor hanging back.

"Thanks a lot," Rachel said, sounding annoyed.

"What do you mean?"

"You were supposed to be showing Mom and Dad how cute the puppies are."

"Well, you're doing it. Anyway, no one's watching."

"They might be. They're all inside. They could be looking out the window."

Laurie said to Rachel, "No, my sister's here, so they're probably watching her kids."

Zanna headed for the water tub just inside the gate to the yearling pasture. She wanted to give Moss a drink before she put him in the barn. As she reached for the latch, he tried to leap over the gate. She had to yank him hard.

"Tell him to stay," said a voice behind her. It was Janet, Laurie's sister. "I went looking for this dog," she said. "I thought I'd give him a little work."

"Your father just did," Zanna told her. "Awhile ago. To show some people that were looking at a puppy."

"I know." Janet grinned. "Sounds like the usual disaster." She shook her head, and her brown hair, cropped short and close like a cap, lifted briefly and fell back into place.

"So then I took Moss for a walk," Zanna said.

"Good. Poor thing's going stir-crazy."

The moment she released him, Moss dashed into the pasture. Janet ran after him, caught him, and dragged him back. "Stay!" she commanded. Moss stood, leaning toward the sheep. She walked ahead of him, then called him to her. He bounded forward. "Here!" she said, her voice sharp and full of purpose. She made him stand beside her a full minute before casting him off to the right. "Away," she drawled in a low voice.

Off he went, streaking along the fence line. He was more than halfway down the pasture before the yearlings realized he was coming. As soon as they moved, he altered his direction and started to turn in on them.

"Out," Janet shouted at him. "Moss, get back out."

He veered away again, making a wide arc around the sheep and coming in behind them. Then he slowed.

"Lord," Janet murmured. "What a dog!" Next she told him to walk up. The sheep came barreling toward her. "Lie down!" she called to him. When he kept on after the sheep, she began to run toward them and him. That was all it took to make him obey. He dropped in his tracks. She gave him another command— "Come bye"—and he swung wide to his left and advanced toward them from the side. "That'll do," she called. She waited until he had returned to her before praising him. Then she repeated the exercise, this time making him swing to the right to flank and slow the sheep.

Afterward she walked him to the barn, speaking to him all the way. Zanna sat with Moss while Janet took his water bucket away to be rinsed and filled. When they left him, he was lapping noisily, not moping.

As Janet and Zanna emerged into the sunshine, they met their fathers in the barnyard discussing rotted sills and spongy porch steps. "Don't close it all in," Gordon recommended. "Sooner or later I'll dig out under there and fill in some good draining gravel."

Janet cut in. "Dad, we need to talk about me taking Moss."

Gordon's expression took on a pained look. "I've more to worry about than that foolish dog. Anyway, you know it's up to your grandfather."

Janet scowled. "But I'm never sure what he's trying to say. Grandma's no help either. She makes up what she wants to believe he's telling her."

Zanna's dad said, "Claire thinks Rob's communicating better all the time. She says it's important to keep him trying."

Janet nodded. "All right." She turned to Zanna. "Come with me. I need moral support."

Zanna said, "If you take Moss, would you bring him back at all?"

"Of course. I come over regularly anyway, especially to work Tess out here before I trial her. So Grampa would get to see his dog doing what he was born for, not sulking and driving customers away. And making Dad split a gut every time he tries to run the dog."

The Catherwood kitchen was full of people, Rob in his wheelchair drawn up to the table, Janet's two little boys playing on the floor, Dot and Fennella and Zanna's mother sorting out word cards across from Rob. The cards reminded Zanna of when she had trouble learning to read.

Janet pulled a chair from the corner and dragged it over beside Rob. "Grampa," she said, "I want to talk to you about an idea I have." She leaned down to unlock the wheels.

"Don't move him without asking or telling," Fennella instructed.

"Sorry," Janet answered. "Grampa, I need to see your face. Okay?" She swiveled the wheelchair around. "Grampa, I just ran Moss on the sheep. He wasn't anything like what Dad was telling us before."

"Slowly," Zanna's mother told Janet. "Separate your words."

Janet nodded. She leaned toward her grandfather. "That dog is dying to work. I could have him ready for trialing by the end of May."

Rob uttered a string of syllables that sounded like someone gargling. Fennella reached across the table with a cloth and wiped spittle from the slack side of his mouth.

"What do you think, Grampa? Do you want me to try?"

"Aah," drawled Rob. "Aagh."

"You can't take on another dog," Dot objected, thumping her fleshy arms down on the table. "You've already got too much to handle."

"But this is something I want to do," Janet replied without shifting her glance from Rob's face. "For Grampa," she said. "And for Moss."

Fennella stood up. "Rob," she announced in what amounted to a shout, "I'm taking you outside." She always raised her voice with him, as if he were hard-of-hearing. "Rachel and Laurie have the puppies on the lawn. They'll be something to look at." She unlocked the other side of the chair and pulled it away from Janet. "Do you need to pee before you go out?"

"He just did," Dot told her.

Zanna tried to pretend that she hadn't heard this exchange. How could Rob stand everyone talking that way all around him?

As soon as they left the kitchen, Dot turned on Janet. "Can't you see you're getting your grandmother all riled for nothing?"

Janet threw up her hands. "All right. I give up. But it's a waste of a great dog." She sounded disgusted.

Steven, the older boy, looked up at her. "Are you mad, Mommy?"

Janet shook her head. "So I'll drop it," she said to her mother.

And Dot replied, "You know your dad and I are for it. We don't need but one dog around here besides old Queen. Meg works just fine. We certainly don't need one like Moss. Maybe in a while . . ." Her voice fell away.

The smaller boy toddled toward the wood stove. Dot got up to intercept him.

"If you mean in a while when Grandma faces up to Grampa's condition, that may be too late."

Dot pulled the child onto her lap and hugged him. "Some things," she murmured, "can't be helped."

Mom and Zanna said good-bye. They stopped for a moment on the porch before heading home. Mom always made a point of touching Rob, of bringing her face close to his when she spoke to him, even just to say that she would see him later.

"Aah," groaned Rob.

Somehow Mom understood that he wanted her to look at the puppies strewn about below him on the brown lawn.

"Beauties," Mom said to Rob.

Hearing her, Rachel bundled a puppy in her arms, cuddling it like a baby. The look she sent Mom said this was the one she would choose. If she could. If only Mom would relent and change her mind.

"Irresistible," Mom declared, letting Rachel know by her tone that she would resist to the end.

7   The weekend had its ups and downs. Mom worked with Dad to shore up the porch steps. It felt good to Zanna, who kept both her parents supplied with nails and who helped to hold boards up against studs that were almost too soft to support the risers. By the time Rachel came wandering over, with Laurie in her wake, Zanna and her parents were putting the tools away.

"That should hold for a while," Dad remarked. "At least as long as we're here."

"Are we moving again?" Rachel asked.

"Not right away," Dad told her.

"I wish we didn't have to go all the way to California," Rachel said. "All my friends are here."

"You'll make new friends."

"Look," Mom put in, "it isn't happening yet. It may never happen."

Dad sent her a look. "It's getting closer," he said.

Sensing the beginning of a new argument, Zanna went inside and up to her room, where she flopped on her bed with a book. Soon after that she heard Mom's car start up. She hoped Dad was going along to keep Mom company, but she didn't go down to check. Instead she looked at her homework for a while and then read until lunchtime. By then everyone was getting along better again. Even Rachel was in a better mood. She had got Mom and Dad to agree to her joining a drama club that met one afternoon a week after school. Nothing more was said about a puppy.

Saturday night the whole family went into Coventry to meet old friends and go to the movies. Afterward they all stopped for pizza. While Rachel and the older kids talked, Zanna let her thoughts drift again to Moss. It felt good to recall how he had come to her after she had given up, how he had walked beside her, almost willingly.

Sunday morning Mom sat awhile at breakfast instead of hurrying to the farm to give Rob his therapy. She and Dad seemed to be picking up on a conversation that had begun earlier.

"I do understand how you feel about the Catherwoods," Dad said to her. "I just wish you had some idea of how long it will take to see Rob through."

Mom poured second cups of coffee and leaned back in her chair. "I'm not saying I have to stick this out until he walks. Fennella sees every tiny improvement as a step toward complete recovery. Right now she needs that hope. As does Rob. That's why I'm giving him so much physical therapy along with the speech work. I honestly don't know what it will lead to."

"Can Fennella really tell what he's saying?" asked Zanna. She was wondering how much good it would do if Rob were able to walk but still couldn't make himself understood.

"I guess she can figure out some of it," Mom answered. "It would be better for Rob if she pushed him into finding the right words. But I suspect Fennella's been speaking for him all their lives together."

Dad laughed, and Mom laughed with him. They went out for a long walk by themselves before Dad had to leave for the airport.

Zanna clung to him when he said good-bye. "Don't go yet," she whispered. "There's something I want to ask you."

"What?" he said, holding her close.

But her mind went blank. Maybe there hadn't really been anything. "I forget," she told him.

"Speak to you next Sunday," he promised. Away he drove in the rental car.

Mom and the girls stood for a moment watching. Then Mom called for dirty clothes. She would start a wash before going over to the farm to work with Rob.

Rachel followed her into the house. She always had a lot of things for the laundry.

Zanna stayed outside. Now that Dad with all his heartiness was gone, the house would feel empty again. Maybe it was waiting for its own family, for Gordon and Dot and the two of their children who still lived with them. Waiting for them to come home where they belonged.

8

On Monday afternoon Zanna asked the bus driver to drop her off at Ragged Mountain Farm. The driver wasn't sure she should, until Zanna explained that no one was home at her house. Never mind, she thought, that no one was ever home after school. But the bus driver was convinced. She drove on past Zanna's driveway and stopped on the crest, midway between the lower farm and the Catherwood house.

The only person Zanna saw was Rob. She waved to him as she crossed the lawn. Meg came wriggling around her feet. Even old Queen thumped her tail as Zanna stepped past her.

Zanna couldn't go inside to look for Dot or Fennella without first stopping to speak to Rob. She made herself go straight to him and said, "I've come to see if I can take Moss for a walk."

"Ga . . . aah," Rob seemed to reply.

She blurted the truth. "I wish I could understand."

"Mess," he said to her. "Some."

She shook her head to show her bafflement. She tried to meet his eyes, but saliva dribbled down his chin. In spite of her good intentions, she backed away and then planted herself at the door to call Fennella. As soon as Fennella gave Zanna permission, she turned on her heel and ran to the old cow barn, where the puppies seethed around her.

Moss stood up as she went to him. He didn't wriggle like Meg or thump his tail like Queen, but at least he acted as though he knew her. She noted this change with a surge of joy.

Moss was unnerved by the wiggling and fawning puppies. He growled and shrank from them before leaping the barrier and dashing out of the barn. By the time Zanna caught up with him, he was at the pasture gate. He balked when she tried to lead him away. She promised him a walk, promised him she wouldn't chain him up again for a long time. Finally she simply hardened herself against the gagging sounds he made and dragged him off.

She took him on a path that joined the shortcut between the farm and her house. The path continued on into a cornfield. She remembered the chopper out there last fall, the corn shooting out of one machine and into another. As soon as she and Moss stepped through the gap into this field, he tensed up. Maybe he expected all fields to hold cows or sheep.

She tightened her grip on the rope. She had thought they might run together, but the ground between the rows of stubble sank underfoot. She led Moss along the edge, wading through stands of dead goldenrod and milkweed stalks with a few empty pods still attached. Moss sniffed at the stone wall, straining against the rope. Everything engaged him, called to him: woodchuck holes, crows flapping up before them, some small creature in a bare tree that whistled and screeched as though wounded.

Zanna saw how Moss gathered in his surroundings with nose and ears and eyes. And every once in a while he cast a momentary glance her way, as if she happened to appear within the scope of his searching and suddenly he recognized her. Only then did she speak to him. While he was intent on the wall and the field, she didn't intrude.

Longing to set him free, she considered what his life had

become since late last summer. Did he think that he was chained up day after day to be punished? He must wonder why Rob had stopped caring for him. What if every time someone came to release him he believed that his imprisonment was over, that he was forgiven for some wrong he couldn't fathom?

At the upper end of the cornfield Zanna felt as if they were at the top of the world. But there, beyond the wall, hayland climbed still higher to the north and east. The wind made a lot of noise up here, rustling dried corn husks that had escaped the chopper and bending gnarled gray branches until they creaked.

As soon as Zanna caught sight of the late bus far below her, she started back downhill. By the time she neared the pasture and barns, she didn't think Moss would get into trouble if she let him go. But the moment he was free, he charged toward the pasture gate.

"No!" she yelled at him. To her amazement he stopped. But only for an instant. Then he took off for the front of the house. She knew he was heading for the porch and Rob.

When she caught up with him, Moss was already ensconced, pressed against Rob's legs, his muzzle thrusting at Rob's hands. They seemed to fly apart, the left one blocked by the chair arm, the right one flopping over the side.

"Aah," moaned Rob, "aah, sliver."

Zanna darted forward to block the fall. It all happened too fast for her to consider the awfulness of touching the paralyzed arm. She grabbed Rob's hand, just as it slid off Moss's shoulder. Then, instead of returning the hand to Rob's lap, she placed it on the dog's head.

She glanced guiltily toward the door, but no one seemed to be nearby. She thought about the word Rob had spoken, *sliver*, and wondered what he had meant by it. She guessed that he had feared the pain of his arm dropping down. Or maybe he had felt it, crying out as he did.

"Moss had a walk," she said to Rob. "Now he has you. He must be happy."

Rob uttered syllables she couldn't understand. Keep going, she told herself. Talk to him. "When he gets to know me, when he comes when I call him, maybe then I'll be able to let him go."

"So . . ." Rob replied. Or was it "Sew?"

While she tried to think of more to say, Rob went on. "Doog, doog. God."

She figured that *doog* meant "dog." She tried that out, her voice rising on a questioning note.

"So," he repeated, "so."

Even though his voice was nearly expressionless, she took its softness for agreement. She was beginning to detect some differences in the way he uttered his garbled words.

Still crouched close to Moss and Rob, she blurted, "I wish I could talk dog."

Rob tilted back his head as a kind of sob issued from him. She was horrified. What had she done to make him cry?

"What's Grampa laughing at?" asked Laurie as she clattered up the steps and dumped her book bag by the door.

Zanna turned to her. "Is that laughing?"

Laurie nodded. "Hi, Grampa," she said. "Where is everyone?"

"I don't know," Zanna answered. "Moss and I just came back from a long walk."

"Grampa, you need anything?" Laurie scanned the small table where his things were kept. She said to Zanna, "Offer him a drink from that mug with the straw. I'll be right back."

But when Zanna moved, so did Moss. This time she easily rescued Rob's hand as it was dislodged. When she placed it over the other hand in Rob's lap, she felt a drop fall from his mouth to the back of her own hand. To hide the shudder that passed through her, she busied herself with Moss, who rolled onto his back at Rob's feet. Wiping the back of her hand on the dog's flank, she rubbed his upturned belly.

She looked up at Rob. Trying not to notice the wetness on his lips and chin, she said, "He's probably remembering how you used to scratch him. Right?"

Rob grunted some kind of assent.

"He's letting me do it for you," she added. "I think he knows it's for you."

"Some," said Rob, "some."

Laurie slammed out of the house with a fistful of crackers. Zanna stood up, asking whether it would be all right to leave Moss with Rob. Laurie didn't think so. It was coming on to chore time, and everyone would be busy. Moss was bound to get into trouble.

"I don't mind putting him away for you," Laurie offered.

Zanna was tempted. If Laurie took Moss to the barn, Zanna wouldn't be the one to chain him up. Still, she guessed she'd better take care of him herself.

For a moment Moss refused to budge. He seemed glued to Rob. Zanna had to give him a sharp tug before he finally gave in, shook himself, and let her lead him down the steps and around the house to the barn.

9

The weather turned raw. Intermittent rain left the road and driveway slimy.

Zanna didn't think it was quite dark enough to turn on the lights, but it was dismal and murky in the house, and there was nothing to do. She went into the living room and switched on the television. A talk show host plucked speakers out of the studio audience. On the next channel two soap opera women sputtered at each other. Zanna switched channels again and found a game show that reminded her of some of the word cards that her mother tried to get Rob to work with.

At a commercial break she went to find the Scrabble set. Dumping the wooden letters out of the bag, she fished around for the right ones to spell *doog*. It was the first time she had ever handled the Scrabble letters. This was a game for good spellers, for Mom and Dad and Rachel.

She got the first and last letters mixed up, so that instead of *doog* she made *good*. She sat back on her heels and stared at the word she had spelled. Then she switched the first and last letters for *God* and ended up with *dog*. She gazed at each word. "Good," she said out loud, ignoring the laughter and applause blaring out of the television. "Good dog," she declared. Rob had been speaking to Moss then, telling him he was a good dog. Or telling Zanna. "Good dog!" she shouted in triumph. She felt as if she had just cracked a secret code.

She was in such a hurry to try out her discovery on Rob that she forgot her boots. By the time she reached the farm her sneakers were soaked and muddy. She took them off and left them outside the back door.

Everyone was starting out to chores. Meg pranced in front of them. Zanna went on in to Rob, who was in the parlor in front of the television. He was watching the end of the same game show that had led to her discovery about his words.

"Hi!" she greeted him, approaching from behind. "It's me, Zanna."

He didn't stir. Coming around to face him, she dropped to her knees. His head was tilted sideways.

"What you said about Moss," she said. "I think it was about Moss," she added, and then faltered. There was no sign that she was getting through to him. He didn't seem to be watching the television screen either. His eyes were vacant, his face slack.

"Rob?" She tried once again. "I figured out your words."

Nothing changed. Rob might as well have been deaf and blind.

She waited awhile, just in case he came to himself and noticed her. Then she picked herself up. At least there was Moss to visit. Did he expect her to come? She wondered how dogs measured time. Meg was always ready for chores, just as if she could tell time. Zanna supposed that Moss listened to the regular daily sounds that reached him in the barn. Probably he had learned the farm routine before Rob's stroke. And remembered it still. Like Rob, she thought, each of them, man and dog, aware somehow and needing to be where they could not go.

It occurred to Zanna that Moss might be able to catch Rob's attention. She asked Laurie, who was feeding the puppies, whether she could bring Moss to him.

"Don't ask me," Laurie told her with a grin. "If I don't know about it, I can't stop you. Just make it quick," she advised.

Moss was already on his feet, his eyes on Zanna, his tail waving slowly. She grabbed a loop of baler twine to slip through his collar. Rachel and Laurie distracted the puppies while Zanna and Moss ran past them and out of the barn.

In the back entry she kicked off her wet sneakers and used her jacket to wipe off Moss's paws. Then he made a beeline for the parlor. How did he know Rob was in there? Was it the television that told him?

Rob was asleep, unreachable. His head, more tilted than before, looked as if it were set wrong, the right shoulder sagging, the right side of his face drooping. His left side seemed to be waiting for the right side to catch up.

Moss leaned against Rob, his muzzle upthrust, his eyes seeking contact with Rob's. Zanna thought how glad Rob would be if he woke up now. She reached past the dog and turned off the TV. Rob slept on. She bent her face to Moss's head. "Good dog," she whispered into his ear. "Doog," she murmured. "God."

After a while she tugged Moss away from Rob. She padded

through the kitchen to the back entry, where she struggled again with her sneakers. Then she let Moss outside and allowed him to lead her around as he sniffed here and there and shook himself a lot. The rain came down more steadily, drenching them both, until it seemed that even Moss wouldn't object to the shelter of the barn.

At supper that night she asked Mom whether Rob was going deaf.

Mom didn't think so.

"He acted like he didn't hear me," Zanna went on.

"He's depressed," Mom told her. "Mood swings are common with stroke victims."

But Zanna had heard her say that about girls Rachel's age, too. "I thought he was getting better," she said.

Mom nodded. "When he's depressed, he slips." She paused. "I'd like to have known him before. I get the impression that he was kind of slow and deliberate on the surface, but with a quick wit inside." She shook her head. "I don't see that in Gordon. Maybe it skips a generation."

"What do you mean?" Zanna asked her.

"That Laurie or Dave might be like him," Rachel answered for Mom.

"Maybe," Mom said. "Janet seems to take after her grandparents."

"Who do I take after?" Zanna asked.

But before Mom could answer, Rachel said, "I take after Mom." She sounded pleased about it.

"You have your grandmother's red hair," Mom said to Zanna. "Maybe you have some of her other traits as well."

"But her hair's gray," Zanna objected.

Mom shook her head. "No, I mean your father's mother. She had red hair, and . . . well, you look a bit like her."

Zanna pondered looking like Dad's mother, who died a long

time ago. She wanted to know who she took after that was alive, like maybe Dad. But she let the matter drop. There was so much else to think about just now. If only she had let Moss wake up Rob, so that they would have had their visit together. She had let the moment pass. Moss had had no response at all from Rob, and Rob had slept right through a waking that might have gladdened his heart.

10

The bad weather continued. Drizzle turned to sleet and then, for a while, to snow. But there wasn't enough for fun.

On Sunday, when Zanna and Moss came back from a long tramp through the woods, Janet was working her dog, Tess, on the yearling ewes. Moss charged up to the gate and cleared it. Zanna's shout had no effect on him, but Janet was able to make him lie down inside the pasture. Then she went on working Tess. Janet used a whistle to direct her dog. There was a different sound for each command.

Zanna let herself through the gate and crouched down beside Moss. "I'm sorry," she told Janet as Tess returned, her lesson finished. "I didn't have Moss on the rope because I knew Rob wouldn't be on the porch."

Janet was unfazed. "No harm done," she said. "He's just keen to work. Want to try him?"

Zanna's breath caught in her throat. "Me?"

Janet nodded. "Remember the basic commands. Think of the dog's right. That's 'away to me.' If you want him to go to his left, tell him 'come bye.' When you get mixed up, lie him down and take some time to figure out what you want him to do."

Zanna nodded. "How did you get him to stay still while you were working Tess?" she asked.

"He knows I mean it," Janet answered. "Maybe he guessed he'd get a turn if he behaved. Now tell him to look for the sheep."

But the instant Zanna spoke to Moss, he bounded past her. "No!" she wailed. She turned to Janet for help.

Janet refused to bail her out. "It's up to you to convince him you mean business. So make him lie down."

"Lie down!" screeched Zanna.

Moss streaked on. How could he, after all she had done for him?

"How would you command him," Janet asked in a voice tinged with amusement, "if you saw a truck ahead of him and you knew he would be hit if you didn't stop him?"

"Moss!" Zanna bellowed. "Lie down!" She was staggered to see him drop in his tracks. "Now what?" she asked.

"Moment of truth," said Janet. "Make him stay while you go to him."

"All that way? Can't I just call him back and start over?"

"What then? Praise him for coming? He needs to learn that you won't put up with what he did. Run out to him while he still remembers everything he did wrong. Drag him back here."

So Zanna set off. She was out of breath as she neared him. He sprang out of reach. Suddenly she was furious. "You stay there," she gasped. "You—you—" she sputtered. He shrank from her fury, turning his face away as she grabbed him. She didn't have to drag him, though. He came right along with her, tail down, ears flat back.

When she told him to look for the sheep again, he ducked his head, eyeing her first before setting his gaze on the yearlings at the far end of the pasture. Starting off, he seemed unsure of himself. Or was he unsure of her? But as he gained on the sheep, he widened out behind them. Zanna was so struck with the beauty of him that she forgot she had to give him another command.

"Lie down," Janet reminded her quietly.

"Lie down!" Zanna repeated at the top of her lungs.

Moss dropped to the ground, then instantly rose.

"Tell him to walk up," Janet advised. "If he speeds up, lie him down again to remind him he's bringing the sheep to you."

Zanna called Moss onto the sheep. Never mind that he was already moving them toward her. She kept expecting him to lose control the way he had with Gordon, but nothing of the sort happened.

When the sheep drew close, Janet told her to shift her own position and flank Moss to the side to slow and stop them. But as soon as Zanna moved, she broke her concentration. Stumbling over the flanking commands, she told Moss to go right when she meant left. Instead of correcting herself, she froze. But Moss responded to her body motion rather than to the spoken word. Astonished and humbled, Zanna just stood there in a maze of confusion.

Janet was laughing. "That's enough for a first try," she told Zanna. "Tell Moss, 'That'll do.'"

Zanna had to say it twice before he was willing to quit. She watched with admiration and envy as Janet released Tess with a quiet word.

"So how did that feel?" asked Janet, closing the gate behind them.

Zanna, who had stopped to give Moss a hug, which he deigned to accept in his detached way, didn't know how to answer. She felt shy about the excitement that had seized her. She felt dumb about getting mixed up. "How did he know what to do when I gave him the wrong command?" she asked.

"A good sheepdog always places himself so that he holds the sheep to the handler," Janet told her. "He knows by instinct where the pressure is, where the sheep want to break away. If you'd kept moving, he would have kept shifting to keep the sheep between you. Moss can teach you a lot because he has so much natural balance. Practice often, but never for long."

"You mean I can do it again?" Zanna blurted.

"Sure. Preferably after you've had him out for a run first."

"I can work him when you're not here?" Zanna exclaimed.

There was only a slight pause. "I'm pretty sure you can. We'll check with Grampa."

After Zanna had put Moss away and Janet had gathered up her little boys from the puppies, they went inside. Janet drew up a chair so that she could face Rob while she told him about Moss and Zanna's first working session.

"Aah," said Rob, "doog, doog."

"Dog, yes," answered Janet. "Moss."

Zanna crouched, almost dog level, and looked up into his face. "Good," she said, "very good."

He looked down at her, compressed his lips as the spittle formed, and then nodded, nodded.

"Moss was a good dog," she said to him, separating each word for emphasis.

Rob nodded again.

"There you go," said Janet afterward as she bundled the boys into her van. "You're over the first hurdle. When I come next Sunday, I hope you'll have something to show me. And a whole lot of questions."

As soon as Janet was gone, Zanna felt like running back to the house and going through that exchange with Rob once again, just to be sure. But Fennella was probably with him now. Zanna decided to wait for some time when she was alone with Rob, when no one else would hear if she turned out to be all wrong.

At least he was listening again and trying to be understood. Maybe he would find a way to let her know that she had guessed right about *doog* and *god*. Dog talk, she thought, dog talk of a sort.

1 The school bus turned onto Ragged Mountain
Road. Zanna couldn't wait to get to the farm.
Spring was in the air today, and she could see a green tinge in
the steeply sloping fields in spite of the snowy patches that clung
to the shaded hollows. Maybe she would take Moss this way on
their walk, only not too close to the highway.

Lately he had been challenging her, time after time forcing her
to make him obey. Fennella thought he was out of sorts because
the puppies had grown bolder and were beginning to pester him.
A few had already gone off to their new homes. As soon as the
rest of them went, he would be left in peace at the end of his
chain. But Zanna wondered whether the little bit of work they
did together made him crave more activity, more freedom.

The bus jolted to a stop.

"Sheeps!" the driver announced.

Zanna peered out the windows. The sheep were cropping
weeds sheltered in the ditches that bordered the road. "Maybe
they're being moved," she suggested doubtfully. Only wouldn't
Meg be with them? "You'd better pass them," she told the driver.
"I'll get the Catherwoods."

The driver inched the bus along until it was safely past the
sheep. Zanna was relieved to see that there weren't any lambs
among them. That meant this was the pasture flock, yearlings
and ewes whose lambs had already been sold. But how had they
gotten all the way down here?

As soon as she was dropped off across from the farmhouse, she
started calling Fennella and Dot and Gordon. No one answered.
Someone had to be nearby, because there was Rob on the porch.

She dashed around to the back, still calling. Queen, lying in a
bar of sunshine, whacked her tail as Zanna charged past her.
There was still no sign of Meg.

All Zanna could think of was how easily the sheep could wander down to the highway. Cars and trucks speeding along were bound to hit some of them.

As she stood in the barnyard, a plan formed in her head. If it went wrong, it would be her fault. But if she did nothing, it might be a lot worse.

The remaining puppies scrambled to greet her. Moss growled as he ran through them. Outside he headed for the pasture gate.

"No! Lie down!" Zanna ordered.

He faltered, glanced at her, and took another step. She ran and grabbed his collar. Leading him down to the road, she turned him so that they both faced toward the highway. On their right and above them stood the farmhouse and the old barns. On their left, and well below the road, clustered the silos and pole barn and milking parlor. If only someone would appear from either side and take over.

Zanna had to decide on the best direction to send Moss. On the house side the fence would keep him close to the road. If he moved straight toward the sheep, he might push them ahead of him onto the highway. On the dairy side the wooded stretch dropped off so steeply that Moss would be out of her sight. Could she trust him to swing wide enough to get all the way around the sheep without startling them?

Zanna scanned the house and barns one last time. The place seemed empty, except for Rob in his wheelchair up there on the porch. Had he seen the sheep get out? Could he tell what she was up to now with Moss?

Thrusting Moss left, she told him to come bye. Loose gravel sprayed up as he scooted off. When she saw how wide he was going, she was elated. But as soon as he plunged into a gully, she wished she had sent him to the right, where she could have kept track of him. Did he have any idea where the sheep were? What if he turned to the road too soon and the sheep bolted away downhill?

All Zanna could do was pelt along the road. Maybe if Moss cut in, she would be able to stop him and prevent a disaster. Skidding on stones and sheep droppings, she passed her own driveway. Now she had to slow down until the road leveled off. She could see nothing. Panic drove her into running again. She could hear her feet pounding on the treacherous road. Or was it her heart banging in her chest? Rounding the long curve, she saw sheep ahead, twenty or so, still more or less together, still safe.

A few of the nearest ones looked up at her. Afraid of spooking them, she came to a full stop. After a long moment she caught sight of Moss before any of the sheep noticed him. He was creeping toward them on the crown of the road, dead center. Zanna was spellbound, thrilled by the dog's stealth and absolute control. He seemed to sense that this was real work and there could be no room for nonsense. He knew exactly what he was doing.

She stifled an impulse to call to him. Any word, even praise, would distract him. Instead she began to scramble backward up the road. Slowly, slowly, the sheep drew together under the pressure of Moss's intense approach. Soon the flock was turned. Like a rippling wave, it tumbled toward her. Moss was the steady wind that drove it home.

As the pace quickened, Zanna struggled to stay ahead. If only she could think of a command to slow Moss down and keep him back. No words came into her head. So the sheep moved on with increasing roughness, some on the fringe skittering off to the side.

Every runaway was a challenge to Moss, who kept flanking to keep the flock together, to keep the wave rolling on.

A truck approaching from the opposite direction pulled into

the farm driveway. Turning, Zanna caught a glimpse of Gordon and Meg jumping down from the cab. At the sight of the oncoming sheep, Meg dropped to the ground, eyeing them.

"What's going on here?" Gordon shouted.

Fennella, her head wrapped in a towel, came around from the back door. She called to him that the sheep must have broken out of the pasture. They needed to be put somewhere safe until the fence was fixed.

Gordon ran to the side of the barn and slid open a door. Then he sent Meg to collect the sheep. "Lie down!" he bawled at Moss, who had no intention of yielding up his found flock. "Get that dog out of here," he yelled at Zanna. "We don't need him messing up."

Zanna was able to grab Moss. She held him close. He was panting hard, his eyes riveted on the sheep that Meg was forcing into the barn. "You didn't mess up," she told him. "You were wonderful." No one would ever know how wonderful. Except maybe Rob. At least he had witnessed the start of Moss's gather and some of the end.

Proudly she led Moss up onto the porch. He leaned against Rob's legs, too spent to try climbing into his lap. "Moss didn't mess up," Zanna declared to this man who couldn't respond. "It isn't fair. He fetched the sheep all this way and wasn't allowed to finish." Tears stung her eyes. What was the point of telling Rob? What could he do about it?

He moved in the wheelchair as if he were trying to straighten his paralyzed side. He strained back, fixed Zanna with a look, opened his lopsided mouth, and in a high, strange voice droned, "Oh Suzanna, oh don't you cry for me. . . ."

Moss pressed his chin on Rob's knee and stared up at him. Zanna just gaped, speechless.

"Suzanna," Rob repeated in that unearthly wail, "don't you cry."

Zanna tasted salt. She shut her mouth. Rob was sort of wheezing now. Zanna could hear Gordon and Fennella shouting back and forth. Was it possible that they hadn't heard Rob sing? Was Zanna the only one, just as she was the only person to have seen Moss rescue the sheep? She faced him squarely. "You sang," she said.

Rob seemed surprised and a little bewildered. Everything drooped now as if something strong had gone out of him. The right side of his face was baggy and wrinkled.

Zanna shook her head. "You did. You sang. To me," she added. Overwhelmed, all she could do was lean against the dog that leaned against the man and wait for Fennella to come.

2

Fennella leaned over to touch Rob's hands. She draped a blanket around his shoulders. Then she yanked the towel off her head and shook her cap of gray hair.

"I was on the bus," Zanna tried to explain. "The sheep were coming down the road. I couldn't find anyone."

"I was in the shower," Fennella answered. "Dot's at Janet's. Gordon was away."

"He blamed Moss," Zanna said. "It wasn't Moss's fault the sheep got out. Moss brought them home."

Fennella glanced down at the dog at Rob's feet. "Gordon sometimes jumps to conclusions. He's come to expect trouble from Moss." She bent to Rob. "You all right if I go look for the fence break?"

"Aah," said Rob.

But he could speak, thought Zanna. He had just sung. Didn't Fennella know?

"Want to come with me?" Fennella asked Zanna. "I might need help."

Zanna nodded. "Can I bring Moss?"

Fennella cast a quick glance around before saying yes. As they walked the fence line, Moss and Meg chased each other in ever-widening circles. This was the kind of fun Moss needed, thought Zanna. She asked Fennella why Gordon didn't like him.

Fennella marched on, her eyes on the fence. Finally she spoke.

"Moss was coming on something grand when Rob had his stroke. But he was Rob's dog only, not like Meg, who'll work for anyone. Gordon can't put up with that. He's short on patience these days, what with all Rob's work to do on top of his own. And the truth is, Moss can act crazy. He can," she added, as if Zanna had objected, "especially in thunderstorms or if someone's hammering metal. Moss will take off and dig himself in somewhere. He even drove Rob wild with worry a few times. Gordon can't stand a dog like that."

There was nothing Zanna could say to all this.

"There," Fennella declared, pointing to a tree lying across the fence. "Those shallow-rooted trees always manage to land on fences. I'll go back for the tractor."

Zanna watched the dogs tussling like puppies. Each time one broke free, there was a brief chase that ended once again in a tangled heap.

Fennella drove the tractor into the pasture and over to the fallen tree. She had a chain saw and tools and chains in the bucket. As she cut away branches, Zanna dragged them aside. After Fennella had cleared enough space to get close to the trunk, she straddled the downed wire and began to cut into the wood. When she made a second slanting cut, the trunk cracked. Fennella raised the saw and stepped clear just as the top half of the tree slumped to the ground. Next she hooked a chain around it and hauled it away from the fence. After that she cut limbs to prop up broken fence posts. And finally she crimped the sagging wire with her fencing pliers. "That'll do till we sink new posts," she declared. "The sheep won't guess how flimsy it is."

Meg and Moss came trotting over. Zanna guessed they had heard Fennella say, "That'll do," about the fence and thought she was speaking to them.

On the way out of the pasture on the tractor Zanna plucked up courage to ask if Moss could help with the sheep. Fennella scanned the area again as if checking to be sure Gordon wasn't around.

"You and Moss keep the sheep from heading for the road," she said. "I'll use Meg to bring them out of the barn."

Standing partway down the lawn, Zanna realized that once again she and Moss were in Rob's line of vision. When the sheep filed out of the side door, they milled about for a moment. Then they took off. Meg dashed around to head them. But that was supposed to be Moss's job. He seemed to think so, too, because he dived at them before Zanna could think of the right command. The flock split.

"Get back," Fennella yelled at him. Meg heeded her command, but Moss remained, his head swinging from one group of sheep to the other.

"That'll do, Moss. Here," Zanna called to him.

Still eyeing the sheep, he backed off. The two groups flowed together.

"Away to me," Zanna told him. "Away, easy."

Moss flanked to the right. But the sheep were rattled, and he was too close for their comfort.

Zanna wasn't flustered anymore. She was just discouraged, because now, when there was someone to see him working, he was all wrong. Still, he edged the sheep toward the gate until they saw the opening and turned into the pasture.

After closing the gate, Fennella tartly praised Moss for pulling himself together after all. Zanna, running to join them, said, "I always think I know the right words until I need them."

"Then you have something in common with Rob," Fennella replied.

Zanna watched Meg take off for the lower farm.

"She knows it's milking time," Fennella remarked. "A real all-around dog, for farm and trials."

"Did you ever run a dog in a trial?" Zanna asked her.

Fennella shook her head. "Not me. Mind you, I was working dogs before Rob ever gave them a thought. I grew up on an island with hundreds of sheep. My father was the lighthouse keeper. We used a dog to round them up twice a year. I showed Rob a thing or two in those days. But I'd freeze up in front of an audience. I would."

Zanna couldn't imagine Fennella freezing up anywhere. "Did you like watching him at trials?"

Fennella heaved herself up onto the tractor. "Indeed I did. I never tired of seeing him handle a dog he loved. Never." She backed and headed down to the road, leaving Zanna to put Moss away in the old cow barn.

3

Mom, who had worked an extra shift yesterday, was sorting through two days of mail. While Zanna tried to tell her about Moss and the runaway sheep, Mom looked at her watch and frowned. It was late. She'd better get over to work with Rob.

Zanna followed her into the front hall. "I wasn't finished."

"Not now," Mom told her.

So Zanna tried another approach. "Can Rob sing?" she blurted.

That did catch Mom's attention. "You heard him sing?"

"Yes. I think so. Yes. Anyway, I thought it was singing."

Mom nodded. "Interesting. Some people with left-brain damage can sing even though they don't speak. I wonder what set him off."

"What I was telling you about Moss and—"

"Tell me later, dear," Mom said, nearly bumping into Rachel, who was coming through the door.

"You should come straight home," Mom snapped at her. "You spend too much time at the Catherwoods'."

"What's eating her?" Rachel asked as the door closed behind Mom.

"I don't know."

"It's probably to do with Dad. There was a letter from him yesterday."

"That ought to make her feel good," Zanna responded, "not bad."

"You're kidding! You mean you don't know what's going on?"

Zanna shook her head. She had no idea what Rachel was driving at.

"You know what a trial separation is?" Rachel asked her.

"I think so. Not exactly."

"It's when a couple splits. Like Amy Levering's folks. They're living apart to see if they like it. Amy goes to her father every other weekend. If they get divorced, she might have to choose who she wants to live with."

Zanna's mouth went dry. It took a moment before she could say, "Dad's away for work. Anyway, he was just home. He wanted to be with us."

"I know," Rachel agreed. "I shouldn't have said anything. You stay cool. If you ask Mom questions, you could make it worse."

That night in bed Zanna tried to summon memories of Mom and Dad happy together. The old ones from when they lived in Prescott Falls brought the most comfort. But even last fall, after they had moved to Ragged Mountain, there had been good times, like swimming in the Catherwoods' pond, with a cookout afterward. Or before that when they all had gone to the Coventry Fair. What a blast that had been, with rides and souped-up cars and the pig scramble and the oxen pulls. Mom and Dad had watched the sheepdog trial for a long time, even though they didn't yet know the Catherwoods.

Zanna kept calling up those memories to keep other ones from surfacing. But she couldn't banish the bad ones, Mom and Dad lashing out at each other or caught in one of their deadly silences.

At some point during the night Zanna heard wind and heavy rain. But that wasn't what kept her wakeful and restless. Her head was full of warnings, danger signals that had escaped her notice until now.

The morning darkness deceived her. Suddenly Mom was at her door.

"You're not up? You'll miss the bus."

Zanna stumbled out of bed. On her way to the bathroom she heard Mom blasting Rachel for oversleeping, too.

Mom, who had just come back from Rob's early-morning therapy, was worried about being late for work. "Hurry!" she shouted on her way to her room to change.

When it was clear that Mom would have to drive the girls to their schools, Zanna was relieved. She wouldn't have to stand out on that muddy road in the driving rain. And now there was time for breakfast. She dropped a frozen waffle into the toaster.

The rain didn't let up until midday. Zanna decided it wouldn't be too wet to take Moss out, but when she went to the barn, he wasn't there. Running to the house, she met Dot, who told her Moss must have taken off during the night.

"But wasn't he chained?" What if Zanna hadn't hitched him properly?

"Storms make him crazy," Dot said. "He broke his collar."

Zanna trudged home. It seemed to take forever before she heard Rachel's bus stop. "Moss is gone," Zanna called to her on the driveway.

Rachel kept on walking. "So are most of the puppies."

"Not sold," Zanna retorted. "They'd never sell Moss. He's Rob's special dog. But he's missing."

"Oh," Rachel answered. "You want to come over to Laurie's? I'm just leaving my stuff and going."

Zanna shook her head. "No one knows where he is," she said.

"So then there's nothing they can do about it," Rachel pointed out as she detoured into the kitchen. "There's never anything to eat around here," she complained. "Come on, the Catherwoods always have good stuff."

But Zanna didn't feel like being at the farm with Moss gone and everyone too busy to care. She followed Rachel to the porch and sank onto the steps.

Small gray and brown birds twittered as they probed the mud puddles left by the storm. Crows rasped in the bare treetops, exchanging strident messages. Or were they quarreling? As Zanna listened to all the clamor, a softer sound came to her, rhythmic and breathy. Rising, she stepped down. The new sound was gone.

Zanna sat back down. The birds were so frantic it was hard to believe they could swallow anything. Keeping her eye on just one, she saw its throat pulse when it raised its beak. While she watched, the soft sound resumed. Not distant. Maybe it came from the cellar. She closed her eyes to listen as hard as she could. The sound was right underneath her, down behind the steps.

Zanna dropped to the ground and peered through the opening Dad had left at the side. She made out some kind of metal thing, maybe a mailbox. Yes, and a large boot near it. But it was too dark to see much more.

She ran inside to get a flashlight. When she crouched again at the opening, she beamed the light toward another shape that looked like a sack of something until it shifted. Drawing back, she took a moment to consider what sort of sack might move. She decided maybe it hadn't and shone the flashlight into the darkness again. This time there was a glint. Two glints.

One night last fall she and Dad had picked up glints like these, glints staring right at them. Dad had said it was a raccoon, but all she had seen were those eyes. After the animal had slipped away, Dad had said good riddance, because it was after the hens.

Now, without Dad or anyone else for company, Zanna wasn't sure she wanted to discover what animal these glints belonged to. She waited. Then she waved the beam back and forth. When she caught the glinting spots again, she held the flashlight steady. She was looking at eyes she knew. There below them was the unmistakable speckled muzzle.

"Moss!" she gasped.

It felt like a miracle. He wasn't just all right. He was here.

If only she had known this morning. She thought of clattering down the steps with Mom and Rachel. All that racket must have freaked him out.

Never mind. His ordeal was over. They had found each other.

4

Zanna's elation soon gave way to frustration. She couldn't get Moss to budge. She tried commanding him with authority. She tried pleading. She even tried tricking him by mentioning sheep. Finally she resorted to bribery with a slice of bread. Never mind that Janet had told her never to use food as a reward. Zanna was out of options.

But when she thrust the bread toward him, he only cowered. So she tossed it down beside the mailbox. At this sudden invasion of his safe zone, Moss lurched back under the darker recess of the porch. She realized she would have to go in after him. That meant pulling at least one board loose, one that Dad had just nailed on.

But then she found that the nails were pounded in so hard that she couldn't pry them loose with the hammer's claw. The more she dug at them, the deeper Moss shrank into the darkness. At last she managed to raise one board with the nails embedded and now somewhat bent. She squirmed through the gap. Finally she was with Moss, more or less, along with the mailbox and the boot. He was panting hard and so tightly wedged in that he couldn't turn from her.

She spoke his name over and over. She might as well have been a stranger to him. Because she was crawling? Because he hadn't yet got over the fright that had propelled him here? When he still refused to come to her, she twisted around and squeezed out. Then she went into the house to call the Catherwoods.

Laurie, who answered the phone, said she would be sure to tell her mother and grandmother where Moss was. She also warned Zanna not to mention his running off to Rob, who didn't know the dog had been missing.

Zanna had a feeling that no Catherwood would be coming after Moss for a while. She didn't mind waiting, though. That would give him time to calm down. And maybe if she kept on talking to him through the steps, he would trust her enough to come out on his own. That would be a whole lot better than having someone who didn't even love him drag him out against his will.

When Zanna heard a car turn into the driveway, she hoped it was Fennella rather than Gordon. But it was Mom, not a Catherwood, who drove up to the house. Mom home with two frozen dinners and a headache. Telling Zanna she was going to lie down before giving Rob his therapy, she said the girls could have their dinners whenever they felt like it.

Zanna figured Moss must be good and hungry by now. She tore open one frozen dinner and slid the tray into the microwave. A few minutes later she shoved the trayful of beef and noodles and gravy under the porch steps. The tantalizing aroma worked. Moss edged toward the food. She withdrew the tray, picked up one slice of beef, and extended it toward him. He stretched forward. The moment she let the beef fall, he snapped it up.

"Good boy," she told him, offering him another slice. This time he took it from her hand. He even licked her fingers neatly, quickly. After that she shoved the whole tray toward him. He started to back away, then stretched toward it and gobbled the remaining food. Then he cast Zanna an expectant look. Maybe he was thirsty.

On her way into the house for water, she stopped to answer the phone. It was Rachel calling to say she was having supper at the farm. Zanna thought hard about Rachel's frozen dinner, but she didn't have the nerve to take it. Instead she slapped together a peanut butter and jelly sandwich for herself and then a second one, in case Moss showed any interest in hers.

Zanna went back to Moss with a saucepan of water and the two sandwiches. He went straight for the water, lapping and lapping until it was all gone.

"I'll get more soon," Zanna promised through a mouthful of sticky peanut butter. When she offered him the other sandwich, he nudged it and then sank down with an injured look.

"You can have some cereal and milk," Zanna told him. "There's no more beef."

Moss licked one forepaw. He seemed to be letting her know that if she couldn't come up with anything better, he would content himself with a leftover drop of gravy.

"Why don't you just come on out of there?" she asked. "The

storm's all gone." But Moss made no move toward the opening, even though it was easier for him to get through now than when he had squeezed in.

Zanna was just going inside for more water when her mother called down to ask what was going on.

"Rachel's at the Catherwoods' for supper," Zanna called back. Maybe this was a good time to tell Mom about Moss. Zanna poured orange juice into a glass and carried it without too much sloshing to her mother, who was lying facedown on her bed.

"What?" she mumbled without looking up.

"I brought you some juice," Zanna said.

Groaning, Mom raised her head and told Zanna to leave it on the bedside table. "That was nice, dear," she managed to add.

Zanna glanced around the room, which was unnaturally dim because Mom had pulled the curtains. Zanna's eye fell on the picture of Dad on the bureau. Would Mom keep it there if she were separating from him?

"Had your supper yet?" Mom mumbled.

"Yes," Zanna replied. "Mom, guess what? I found Moss under the porch."

"Um," murmured Mom into her pillow.

Zanna leaned against the doorjamb. "I didn't know what to do."

"Um," Mom said again. "Probably the rain."

What exactly did Mom mean? Zanna shrugged and went down to the kitchen to fill a bowl with cereal and milk. Moss made short work of it. Then he heaved a sigh and flopped down. He didn't look scared anymore, but he didn't act ready to come out from under the porch steps either. At least he didn't seem about to run off again.

A little later, when Zanna went upstairs, Mom asked her to call the farm and tell Fennella that she couldn't make it tonight.

Fennella should get Rob to practice his tongue exercises, the *oo* and *ow* sounds.

Zanna figured that by tomorrow Mom and Moss and every-thing else would be back to normal. Then Mom would talk to her and Moss would show that he was glad to see her. Meanwhile, it was just fine to know that he was safe and fed and easing up.

Zanna didn't really mind that the reunion under the porch steps hadn't worked out like a Disney movie. It would have been thrilling if Moss had hurled himself at her or even just given her some sign of recognition. What counted was that he was re-turning to himself—and to her. All he needed was a little more time.

5 In the morning Mom was still in bed. She told Rachel to call and tell Fennella she was sick.

Zanna ran outside to Moss. When at first she peered under the steps and couldn't see him, she figured something had made him retreat still farther under the porch. Then she caught sight of the slightly mauled peanut butter sandwich and suspected he wasn't there at all.

Just then Rachel called down to her to say that Moss had shown up at the farm. Zanna pulled back. She shoved the loose board back in place. The nails would have to be straightened. Later. She'd better not miss the bus today.

When she came home from school, Mom was still in bed. Zanna hung around in case Mom needed something.

Rachel arrived late and full of excitement. She had tried out for a big part in a play. Rushing upstairs to tell Mom, she returned to the kitchen with a scowl on her face. Since no one seemed interested in her news, she'd take herself over to the Cather-woods'.

Guessing that Rachel wouldn't stay at the farm for supper two nights in a row, Zanna started to hunt up something that would be easy to fix. She had her head in the refrigerator when Dot barged into the house and up the stairs, calling, "Claire, I'm coming up to see you." Dot stayed up with Mom awhile. When she came back down, she informed Zanna that Mom had agreed to let both girls spend tonight at the farm.

"She shouldn't be alone," Zanna objected.

"Alone is just what your mother needs," Dot retorted. "Anyway, I'll be coming back later with soup and the cordless telephone."

So Zanna gathered up a few things for overnight and her sleeping bag and went along with Dot to the farm.

As soon as she had dumped her things, she took off for the cow barn. Moss lay there on his side, not getting up. But his tail whacked the floor, the white brushy tip stirring up dust and wood shavings from his bedding.

The moment she unhitched him, he was transformed. He raced past the last two puppies with a warning growl and cleared the barrier, which was higher now that the puppies had grown. Outside he darted toward the gate to the pasture. He was after the sheep while she was still shutting the gate behind her. It was clear that everything he had been through had set him back. He could hear only the demon voice that drove him from within. The powerful connection between the dog and the sheep was like a closed circle. It was up to Zanna to break into it and make herself a link between them.

Vaguely aware of someone at the fence watching, Zanna couldn't shake the feeling that Moss sensed that presence, too. He would take advantage of it. Only when there was no one to witness his exploits did he shine.

She had to act as though she were all by herself. So she didn't turn to identify the person at the fence. Scudding across the pasture after Moss, she commanded him to lie down. He ignored her.

When he swung to block a bolting sheep, she met him head-on and clutched him with all her might. "Bad! Bad! Bad!" she scolded as she shook him. All of yesterday's worry and disappointment welled up in her. She was still clinging to the new collar when the sheep took off. Moss lurched, but she wouldn't let him go.

She wasn't sure whether she was taking out her own hurt pride on him or whether this might be one of those moments Janet had warned her about, when a handler could lose the dog she was training. Then, of course, there was the person watching every wrong thing Moss did.

She waited for her breath to return and her heart to stop pounding before she scrambled to her feet and let Moss go. By now the sheep had moved off. When she sent Moss to fetch them, he had to handle them differently because they weren't used to being brought to the top end of the pasture. He had to use his head as well as his instincts. And he had to keep listening to Zanna to complete the gather.

As soon as she told him to stay, she felt the battle raging inside him. She let some of the sheep leak away. He couldn't bear to lose control of them. She spoke his name in a warning tone; now the battle was outside, between the two of them.

Zanna made him lie down. Not trusting him, she swooped to grab his collar again. He flung himself out of reach. "Lie down!" she bellowed in a voice that would have done Gordon proud. Guiltily she glanced down the pasture. Two people were standing there now. She thrust Moss away from the direction he yearned to take, then forced him to stop once more. After that, as a reward, she let him run out to gather the sheep.

Zanna could almost hear Janet reminding her to quit while she was ahead. But now that Moss was holding the sheep quietly and listening again, she wanted to get him driving just enough to prove to herself and to him that they could do it. The sheep moved haltingly because she kept stopping Moss to remind him that he was working for her. Still, the drive stayed straight down the pasture, and when she asked him to turn the sheep, he managed that smoothly, too.

By now he looked ready to explode, so she told him, "That'll do," and stood stock-still until he returned to her. Then she made him walk beside her down the pasture to where Gordon and Mr. Nearing stood talking together by the gate.

"Young lady," Mr. Nearing said to Zanna, "that was quite a show."

She didn't know how to respond. She wanted to get Moss out of the pasture while he still looked good.

"How old are you?" Mr. Nearing asked her.

Zanna told him she was ten and a half.

"A chip off the old block?" Mr. Nearing was addressing Gordon now.

"No," Gordon replied. "A neighbor. Suzanna Wald. Zanna, this is Mr. Nearing, who's come back for another look at the last available puppy." He opened the gate for her and Moss.

Mr. Nearing reached down to shake Zanna's hand. "I'm changing my mind about that dog," he said to Gordon. "If a ten-year-old can get that much out of him, maybe I could try him out. He's more like the way he was with Rob now. I can see that."

"But my father's not ready," Gordon explained. "We can't let Moss go just yet."

"I understand. I can wait, if you think it might work out."

Gordon said, "What about the puppy?"

Mr. Nearing shook his head. "Not if there's a chance for Moss."

Zanna stole a glance at this man. He had the look of someone who was used to getting his way. She couldn't imagine him running after a dog that didn't listen. His clothes looked too good, as if they had come out of a catalog selling rugged outdoor wear. Even his hands were smooth, nothing like Gordon's, which seemed to bear the shape of whatever task they had last performed.

"Are you selling Moss?" she asked Gordon. She could feel the heat rush to her face.

"Maybe," Gordon said. "Not now. We'll see."

Zanna had hoped to take Moss over for a visit with Rob. Now all she could think of was getting him as far away from Mr. Nearing as possible. She looked down at the dog, whose sides heaved as he panted. He was plastered with mud. So she walked him down to the pond, where he plunged in and then stood with the water almost to his back.

"You'd better not run away anymore," she told him. "You better stop jumping gates and stay out of trouble. You hear me, Moss?"

Moss, who was lapping water, stopped to pant, and then lapped some more.

Zanna kept him there, out of the way, until she was pretty sure Mr. Nearing had driven away.

6 All through supper Zanna kept expecting Gordon to mention Mr. Nearing's interest in Moss. The closest the conversation got to it was when Fennella asked Zanna how Moss had behaved that afternoon.

"Usually that dog's all wired after a storm. Isn't that right, Rob?" Fennella speared lima beans and raised the fork to Rob's mouth. She had to shove them in. "You used to have your hands full with him after one of his frights."

"He was bad at first," Zanna said. "But he got better."

"She straightened him out," Gordon put in. "I saw. So did Howard Nearing. He was considering the last pup after all. Then he saw Moss." Gordon paused. "Changed his opinion of him, I guess."

"Does that mean he's taking the puppy?" Dot asked.

But Fennella spoke up before Gordon could reply. "Rob never had much use for that man. Right, dear? Mr. Nearing can buy his way to the top. He's been making offers on Rob's promising young dogs for some years now. He even tried to buy Moss off Rob over to the fair last summer. So he's changed his mind about that dog more than once."

Rob's mouth worked and worked. He could only nod and grunt.

"You've lima beans tucked in on the paralyzed side," Fennella told him. "Move them over."

Rob struggled with his mouthful of food.

"Dad," Gordon said to him, "Nearing called you a living legend. How do you like that?"

"Gaah," Rob responded, and bits of beans dribbled down his chin.

Fennella wiped them up without comment.

After that Gordon got talking to Dave about some milking machine problem. Then they talked about the upland cornfields, which were nearly dried out enough for plowing.

Zanna concentrated on the food, which was plentiful and good. She said yes to second helpings of everything, despite Rachel's glowering signals. Zanna almost explained that she had fed Moss her frozen dinner last night. But since no one else seemed to mind her appetite, she didn't bother to defend herself. At least she wasn't acting weird like Rachel, who seemed so intent on not making a mistake that she ended up stiff as a board. Zanna guessed this was because Dave was there at the table.

Dessert was homemade pumpkin pie. With fresh cream. Dot gave Zanna as big a slice as Gordon's and Dave's. Rachel, who declined even a taste, looked disgusted when Zanna heaped on the cream. But after that, Rachel couldn't keep her eyes off Zanna's plate. Zanna almost felt sorry for her. Rachel was probably dying for some pie, too, but didn't know how to say so now. If that was what falling for a guy did to you, Zanna would steer clear of love.

After supper Gordon and Dave went out together. Dot said she would look in on Claire as soon as she'd helped Fennella get Rob settled in bed. Since Rachel and Laurie declared that they didn't need Zanna helping with the dishes, she wandered into the dining room, which had been turned into the parlor when the real parlor became Rob's bedroom. Zanna's sleeping bag was already laid out on the sofa.

For the first time, she paid attention to the corner cabinet across from the sofa and armchair. It was crammed with trophies. Some had statues of cows, but most showed sheepdogs atop pillars and urns and *Winged Victorys*. All up and down the wall hung plaques inscribed with the names of sheepdog trials and their dates and words like *Champion* or *Reserve Champion*.

Fennella, bringing Rob to his room, paused beside Zanna. She nodded toward the trophies. "Did you know about all Rob's wins?"

Zanna shook her head. She dropped her eyes to Rob. "Did Moss win any of them?"

His mouth twisted. "Tarry," he said. "Some. Tarry."

"The tray," Fennella chimed in. "That one over there. See, Rob was just getting started with Moss. There's ribbons, too. Rob doesn't set much stock in ribbons. He collects the hardware. Don't you, dear?"

Dot spoke from the bedroom. "You coming, Fennella? I should get over to Claire soon."

"We're just showing Zanna the tray Moss won."

"I wish I could do that," Zanna blurted. "I wish I could run Moss in a trial. Until," she quickly added, "Rob can do it again."

"That's an idea," Fennella said. She leaned over Rob's shoulder. "Right, dear? Maybe Zanna could try Moss out in one or two novice classes. Keep him used to the trial scene."

"What's a novice class?" Zanna asked.

"A trial where either the dog or the handler is a beginner."

Rob spluttered before ejecting a few garbled syllables from his mouth.

"One word at a time, Rob," Fennella told him. "I can't make out what you're trying to say."

Rob thrust his head forward, as if to free himself from the chair. "Some, some," he mumbled. "Silo."

"What about the silo?" Fennella asked him.

"Silo," he insisted. "Go. Silo."

Frowning with puzzlement, Fennella shook her head.

Zanna crouched in front of Rob. "Would you let me put Moss in a trial?" she asked. "If Janet said it was all right."

For all of its crookedness, his answering smile told her what she needed to know. Yet he still struggled to get something else across to her. Scraps of words tumbled from his lips. "Some. Some let."

"I expect he's telling you he'll let you do it sometimes," Fennella interpreted.

Rob swung his head to the right and back, his way of shaking it. "Snow!"

Zanna shook her head, too. She was already pretty sure that *some* meant "Moss." She groped for the rest of his meaning. "When Moss lets me? If Moss lets me?"

"Aah," said Rob. "So."

"So," declared Fennella. "That's *yes*. You're right, Zanna. I guess it helps to have a mother who's a speech therapist."

After Fennella had pushed Rob into the bedroom, Zanna wished she had said something about Mr. Nearing. She wanted to hear Fennella declare that even if Mr. Nearing came back with so much money that the rest of the Catherwoods couldn't bear to turn him down, she would never let them sell Moss. It made Zanna uneasy that Gordon hadn't come right out and told everyone about Howard Nearing's intentions. It was too much like Mom not talking about Dad, and Rachel not letting Zanna ask her any questions.

Not that Zanna would have known exactly what to tell Fennella. All she really knew was that something had been set in motion out there at the pasture gate. And what seemed most threatening to Moss was not what the two men had said to each other. It was the unspoken understanding that they seemed to share.

7   Zanna was jolted awake by unfamiliar voices. Well, not exactly unfamiliar, but strange-sounding for the middle of the night. As soon as she remembered where she was, her first thought was that Mom was worse and had called for help.

Zanna felt her way toward the crack of light under the door to the kitchen. Fumbling for the knob, she turned it and then had to squeeze her eyes shut. Adjusting to the brightness, she saw Gordon and Dot in their outdoor things heading for the back door.

"What's happened?" she asked. "Is it my mother?"

Fennella, two mugs in her hands, whipped around, her bathrobe falling open. "Gracious!" she exclaimed. "Did we wake you up?"

"Where are they going?" Zanna demanded. If they were on their way to her house, she wanted to go, too.

"To milk," Fennella told her. "And I'm about to dress and feed the calves and ewes and lambs. If you can't go back to sleep, come along."

Zanna glanced at the kitchen clock. It was a little past four-thirty. "I thought something was wrong with Mom," she said.

"I expect she's having a better sleep than you've had," Fennella told her. "Now I'm going up to the bathroom. Decide what you want to do."

Zanna put on yesterday's clothes and was ready by the time Fennella came downstairs.

"Do you always feed the calves and sheep this early?" Zanna asked.

"Only since Rob came home from the hospital," Fennella said as they stepped out into the cold air. "This way I'm free to help your mother and to learn what I'm supposed to do with Rob during the day. See, Claire gives him physical therapy morning and evening, but she wants his speech exercises going on all the time."

As soon as they switched on the barn lights, the ewes rose, jostling each other. Lambs scrambled underneath them, seeking milk. The ewes crowded forward to get the hay Fennella forked into the racks. When one lamb was nearly trampled, Fennella told Zanna it was a bummer, an orphan, trying to steal a few swallows of milk. Not to worry, said Fennella, the lamb would have its own breakfast in a moment. She showed Zanna the small opening into another pen. The lambs could file through and then spread out at a trough for their feed. The bummer lamb was one of the first to reach it.

Old Queen policed the aisle on the other side of the hayracks. If a ewe stuck her nose in too far, Queen nipped at it.

"That'll do," Fennella said to her from time to time. Queen would back off until Fennella got busy with something else.

"Was Queen a good working dog?" Zanna asked.

"Pretty good. Not as sharp as Meg. We couldn't do without Meg at milking time. And she's won her share of trophies, too."

"Were all Rob's dogs in trials?"

Fennella, who was draining the hose after filling the water tubs, shook her head. "Rob's first dog ever came with me from the island when Rob and I were married. He didn't know a thing then. He was a dairyman. He'd come to judge cows at a fair on the mainland and met one of my brothers, who told him about our island cows and then brought him over for a look."

"That's how you met?"

"That's how we met. And didn't I lead him a merry chase. We had an island roundup. Poor Rob, he had to cover a lot of rough ground that day. Then we put him to work in the sheep pens, sorting lambs for market. That was the first time he saw a dog really working livestock." Fennella paused, remembering. "My brother bet me he'd be back, but a whole year went by. Then he showed up again at fair time and came out to the island to buy a dog. And stayed to learn how to handle her. We left together. Married and left."

Zanna tried to picture Rob and Fennella long ago. All she could do was substitute Janet for Fennella and Dave for Rob. Then she tried to picture the island with the lighthouse and the sheep and dogs. "Do you miss it?" she asked.

Fennella paused again, a forkload of manure suspended. "I miss the sea," she said. "I miss the birdcalls and the smell of rockweed at low tide. And the light on the water, how it changes. We used to talk about going back sometime, but we were always too busy. Now, with Rob like this, I don't suppose I ever will. Anyway," she added, dumping the manure into the wheelbarrow, "it's all changed. The lighthouse went automatic years ago. No one lives there year-round anymore. Two of my brothers still have houses out there for fishing and hunting. They say it's grown up a lot, all black alder and spruce."

Fennella hung up her fork. She was off now to feed the calves. Outside, the sky had turned gray. The house and barn and out-buildings loomed in the morning mist.

"Moss usually gets his run about now," Fennella told Zanna. "I have him back in the barn before I get Rob up. Of course, I make sure Rob gets to see him now and again."

"Was Moss really going to be Rob's best dog?" Zanna asked.

Fennella smiled. "I'll tell you something about best dogs. More than likely they're those that aren't fully trained yet, that haven't been put to the test. Or else they're those that are so long dead that we've forgotten all their faults. You hear about them at the trials, those best dogs. You rarely see them." She swung around. "Well," she demanded, "are you going to let out Rob's current best dog, or am I?"

"I am," Zanna responded, and went flying off to the cow barn. The last puppies had just been moved to a pen near the calves. It seemed empty and lifeless for Moss in his dark corner. He rose and set his tail to wagging, quietly, as if reserving a part of himself that he could not give to her. When she unhitched him, he dashed out without a backward glance.

Zanna slowly followed. She caught a faint whiff of puppies as she passed the place they had bedded. She wondered what Moss had been like when he was fat and fluffy and tumbling over littermates and chewing shoelaces.

She went into the house to warm up and found Dot in the kitchen starting breakfast. Dot had already checked with Claire, who was feeling better this morning. Another day in bed, and she'd be right as rain.

"So what'll it be?" Dot asked Zanna. "Pancakes or scrambled eggs? First kid up gets to choose."

8

Zanna and Rachel spent two more nights at the farm. On Saturday morning they moved back home.

Mom was up and about, but not quite herself. She was worried about Rob's missing so much therapy, but she didn't have the energy to go to him. Besides, she had a pile of paperwork to attend to.

But twice Zanna caught Mom just sitting and staring at the bills, not paying them.

"Are we out of money?" Zanna finally asked.

Mom rubbed her eyes. "I'm just trying to decide which ones can wait."

Pressing for a clue to the separation, Zanna said, "Doesn't Dad send us money?"

Mom nodded. "It isn't anything to worry about." But of course, she was talking about money, not about Dad and her being apart for so long.

Mom went on. "Fennella tells me you've been picking up on some of Rob's mixed-up words. It's funny how some people have a knack for that sort of thing. Maybe you'll be a speech therapist when you grow up."

Zanna shook her head. "I'm going to be a farmer. I'm going to train sheepdogs."

Mom smiled. "I'm glad you had a good time with the Catherwoods."

"I did chores with Fennella."

"Good. I suppose Rachel helped, too?"

Zanna didn't know how to reply. If traipsing around after Dave meant helping with chores, she supposed that was so.

Rachel appeared, as if on cue, to announce that she was going over to Laurie's.

"Don't make a nuisance of yourself," Mom warned in a joking tone.

Rachel flared up. "Is Laurie a nuisance when she's here?"

Before Mom could answer, Rachel was out the door. Mom gave up pretending to do bills and went upstairs to lie down.

Zanna was at a loss. She didn't want to walk out on Mom, too. But after all the busyness at the farm, this house felt lifeless.

She wandered into the furniture room and clambered up onto her bed, where she sat awhile, mulling over the changes in her life during the past few days. While Moss was getting more used to her, she was getting used to Rob, even when he ate and drank. She knew about getting out of the way when he had to go to the bathroom. He needed privacy, even though it took two people to get him on the commode. None of this grossed her out anymore. But there was so much more than not being grossed out. There was the kind of language that she and Moss and Rob were finding together. It didn't depend entirely on words, but the words kept coming.

Zanna was beginning to think that she got so many of them right just because she knew so little. When Rob said, "Silo," for instance, Zanna, who didn't know anything about silos, only heard him struggling to respond to what she had told him about Moss working too close to the sheep. She never saw the word spelled out either. She just heard *slow* in "silo" because it made a kind of sense. When she followed up that word by asking how to slow Moss down, Rob had fixed her with a look that was nearly as intense as a Border Collie's eye. Straining, fighting against wrong syllables, he had finally blurted, "Lie town!" And she had understood what she must do for a start: make Moss lie down.

The front door slammed. Footsteps pounded up the stairs and then down again. Zanna clambered down from the bed and left the furniture room.

"We were looking for you," Rachel told her. "We're going shopping with Laurie's mother. You can come if you want. Mom said so."

"Where?" At least it would be something to do.

"Not in Coventry. Somewhere else. We're taking Janet's van."

"Janet's at the farm?" Usually she came on Sundays.

Laurie nodded. "Are you coming?"

Zanna said no. She ran up to tell Mom she was off to the farm. Mom was looking at a magazine. Her room was a mess, clothes on the floor and cups everywhere. Mom never left clothes lying around.

"I wish you had someone to be with like Rachel does," Mom said. "Next weekend you can have Diane over."

"It's all right," Zanna assured her. "I have Moss."

Zanna ran until she was winded. No one was in the pasture, so she went tearing up to the back door. As she burst inside, she heard Janet and Fennella arguing. Zanna stopped short. Janet and Fennella stopped, too. The little boys went on gabbling.

Fennella turned to Zanna. "What's up? Is Claire all right?"

Zanna nodded. "I just wanted Janet to see how Moss is working." She faltered. She could feel the tension between grandmother and granddaughter. Was there a disagreement over Moss? Maybe it had something to do with Mr. Nearing.

Janet sent her out to get Moss.

"You have to be good," she told him. But he was all steamed up. First he ran circles around her. Then he raced to the gate. "Stay!" she shouted, but he was already up and over. "Lie down!" she yelled. She gave up fumbling with the gate latch and clambered over to descend on him. "Don't you ever do that again," she scolded.

"Lighten up," Janet told her as she unfastened the gate. "After all, he did lie down, even if he was cheating on you in the first place. I'd like to see you encourage him, not pound him."

Zanna's face flamed up. "I usually do encourage him. Lately he's been so good."

"Well, show me," Janet said.

Zanna could barely think. Moss hadn't had a run yet, and now they were off to a bad start.

She had been practicing left-hand outruns because he didn't like going that way. So that was how she sent him now. He tightened as he neared the sheep. "Get back out!" she commanded, her voice shrill with embarrassment. Reacting to her tone, he locked right in on the sheep. He crept so low he looked like a killer, not a herding dog.

If Zanna had been on her own, she probably would have run after Moss as soon as he started going wrong. But now she felt stuck and helpless.

Janet had to prod her into going to him. Close to tears, she thrust him away from the sheep, away from her. Then her mind went blank.

"Back to your starting point," Janet called to her.

Somehow Zanna managed to trudge partway back and make Moss complete his outrun. It was clear that he didn't have his heart in it.

Afterward Janet had a lot to say. "Always start with something you know he can do," she began. "Ease into the hard stuff. That's how you build up his confidence. You have to trust each other."

Trust Moss? How could she when he made a fool of her so often? Zanna shook her head. "He was like the first time I saw him with your dad."

Janet threw back her head and laughed. "That bad?" She was

laughing so hard that her boys, who had been playing near the fence, came over to see what the fun was all about. Janet asked Zanna where she thought things had first gone wrong.

Eager to get something right, Zanna said, "Not noticing when he first started to cut in?"

"Not the dog," said Janet. "You."

Zanna gulped. "I don't know," she mumbled.

"What was on your mind when you sent him out?"

Zanna stared down at the dog, who lay facing the sheep, his ears flat against his head. She could see how miserable he was. Kneeling, she raised his unyielding muzzle and cupped it in her hands. The brown eyes shifted to her face for an instant, then returned their gaze to the sheep. "I wasn't ready," she said. "We weren't ready."

"So why did you send him then?" Janet asked.

"You told me to."

"Zanna," Janet said, kneeling beside her and Moss, "it's between you and Moss. You can tell me to wait." The boys tumbled against her like two-legged puppies.

"I wanted you to see how well he's doing."

"You're a beginner. And he's a young dog that needs a lot of work. More than you know how to give him. He's lost Grampa, who was his best friend. All you and Moss have going for you is the bond you're building between you. Break that, and you're finished."

Zanna nodded. All she wanted to do was get away for a while. She took Moss for a long walk and tried not to think about how she had messed up.

Letting him track new scents, she didn't care where they went so long as he felt his freedom and didn't seem to mind her presence. When the ground began to suck her in with every step, she climbed onto a boulder and sat there, giving him all the time he wanted to plod around in the swamp. When he finally returned to her of his own accord, he was slathered with mud but refreshed and spent. He looked almost glad to find her there waiting for him.

9

On Sunday morning Mom left early to give Rob his therapy. When she was late coming back, Zanna started to worry that Mom had forgotten that Dad always called on Sunday.

Rachel came thumping downstairs in her bathrobe. Usually she took advantage of Mom's absences to get on the phone, but this morning she made no move toward it.

"The phone's free," Zanna pointed out. If Rachel got started talking to one of her friends, Dad would get a busy signal and have to try later. By then Mom was bound to be home.

"No one's up yet," Rachel said with a big yawn. "No one real."

"I bet Dave is," Zanna said.

Rachel gave her a dirty look and headed for the kitchen.

Zanna stared at the phone. She decided to call her friend Diane.

"Do you want to come over next weekend?" Zanna asked.

"Sure," said Diane. "Why are you asking me now?"

"I thought I might forget in school," Zanna told her.

"Oh. Well, see you tomorrow."

To keep Diane from hanging up, Zanna plunged on. "I'll show you Moss. You know, the dog. You can see him work sheep."

"Okay," said Diane.

Zanna was running out of steam. Just then Rachel came through, eating toast and carrying a mug. "Moss is really great," Zanna declared, pumping enthusiasm into her voice to keep the line busy. "I may even get to trial him," she added, unnerved by her own boasting, but unable to stop. "Like at the fair."

Rachel said, "I need the phone."

Zanna nodded. Now she could get off and let Rachel take over.

Rachel pulled the telephone into the closet; that meant she was going to talk about Dave and didn't want Zanna to hear. Dad wouldn't be able to get through now, not for ages.

Mom came in while Rachel was still gabbing away in the closet. "Hungry?" Mom asked. She beckoned Zanna into the kitchen. "I am. First time in days I feel like eating." She hauled fresh milk and eggs out of the refrigerator. "How about French toast?" She broke the eggs into a bowl and began to whip them. "I can't believe how well Rob's doing. I can actually feel some resistance in his right arm during range of motion exercises. And he seems well out of his depression."

The soaked bread sizzled as it was laid in the frying pan.

"Fennella thinks you and the dog have made a difference to Rob."

Zanna rummaged at the back of the refrigerator for the maple syrup. She had an uneasy feeling that Mom was leading up to something.

"Fennella says Janet thinks Moss needs more attention. No one over there has time for him."

Zanna stood half inside the refrigerator. She was terrified of what Mom was leading up to. Thinking of the argument she had interrupted yesterday, she shivered. Was Mom about to tell her that Fennella had changed her mind and would let Mr. Nearing take Moss?

Mom flipped over the French toast to brown the other side. "So Fennella wondered about maybe you keeping the dog here."

Zanna opened her mouth, but not a sound came out. Shutting the refrigerator door, Zanna let out her breath in a long sigh.

"Not for good," Mom quickly added. "Keeping isn't exactly what we mean." When Zanna still only gaped, Mom went on, "He'd be here when you come home from school. You wouldn't be alone." Mom laid out the French toast on two plates. It smelled wonderful.

Zanna found her voice. "What if he doesn't like it here? Will it cost a lot to feed him? Does everyone over there know about this?"

Mom started another batch of soaked bread. She sat down across from Zanna. "The food comes in a big bag from the grain store. We can take what he needs. Fennella expects you to bring him over to Rob a lot. There's no guarantee it'll work out. After all, Moss is a barn dog now. But even Gordon thinks it's worth a try."

Zanna wanted this moment to stretch and stretch so it would last forever—the delicious breakfast together, Mom sounding strong and sure, and the prospect of Moss here all the time. "Can he sleep in my room?" she asked.

"Can who sleep in your room?" demanded Rachel. "Hey, breakfast! Can I have one of these?" She was at the frying pan. While she served herself, Mom explained about Moss.

"What about me?" Rachel drawled. "I was the one that wanted a dog."

"But this is different," Mom told her. "We'll be doing the Catherwoods a favor. With planting starting and haying coming and Dot planning to help out at Janet's stand, no one has time for the dog." Getting up, she fished out the last slice of French toast. "Anyone want more? I can make a fresh batch."

Rachel guessed not. Zanna shook her head. Mom divided the slice into three small portions. Peace descended as they sat finishing the first real meal they had had together in a long time.

"One more thing," Mom said. "Fennella has a not very realistic conviction that Rob can recover enough to work Moss again."

Rachel said, "Not realistic? You don't think he can?"

Mom shook her head.

"But you let her go on believing?" Zanna exclaimed. "How can you?"

"Because it's that kind of hope that keeps him trying. Meanwhile," she added, "I intend to help the family set more realistic goals."

"Like what?" Zanna asked.

"Like Rob being able to speak and be understood where his day-to-day needs are concerned. Like using the urinal by himself, so that he's less dependent on others. Simple but important goals for him."

Zanna couldn't bear to think of the enormous distance these goals were from the one Fennella and Rob had fastened on. When the phone rang, she jumped up to reach it first. "Dad!" she shouted. "I'm getting Moss. When are you coming home to see him?"

"Who?" said Dad.

"Moss. Rob's dog. He'll be partly mine."

Mom was at Zanna's side. "Let me talk first," she said to Zanna, who handed her the phone.

"Barry?" Zanna heard on her way back to the kitchen. "Yes, much better. What about you? Aren't you up awfully early?"

Rachel told Zanna to shut the kitchen door to give Mom privacy.

Zanna said, "She sounds perfectly normal. Like she's glad to talk to him."

"So?" said Rachel. "That doesn't mean anything."

But Zanna was sure that it did. Mom and Dad were apart, but not separated. And everything was going to be as good as it could be with Dad so far away. After all, Moss was coming to stay.

10 Zanna thought all she had to do was run to the farm and fetch Moss out of the barn. No such thing. Moss had to have a flea bath first. That meant taking him down to the lower farm where there was hot water out of the hose. And if one dog was being done, then the others ought to be washed at the same time.

Dave was put in charge. He grumbled all the way to the concrete ramp where the dogs were tied. The cows in the feedlot began to moan. Dave told them to shut up; it wasn't time for milking.

"Don't you like cows?" Zanna asked him.

Dave shrugged. "They're a living. Or used to be. If we did it my way, we'd go into beef." Dragging the hose over to the dogs, he regulated the hot and cold water. Meg and Queen stood patiently while Dave soaked them. "You pour that stuff on them," he instructed. "Suds them good, but don't get any in their eyes."

They submitted to Zanna's scrubbing, but Moss threw a fit. Under the stream of water, he yelped and flung himself at the end of his rope until he seemed on the verge of strangling.

"Crazy, dumb dog!" Dave screamed at him.

Zanna ran to help. But Moss was too frenzied to hear her. His yelping turned to a howl. His eyes bulged; his mouth foamed.

Zanna was scared. "What's the matter with him?" she cried.

"He's just off the wall, that's all. We should've sold him to that Nearing guy while we could."

"You can't. He's your grandfather's."

"Right," said Dave grimly, wrenching Moss around and flipping him on his back. He tossed the hose aside. "That's the best I can do. Get him soaped up. I'll rinse off the others."

Moss was silent now, but trembling. Zanna crooned to him as she rubbed the soap into his coat. He was calmed by the contact and her voice. But as soon as Dave returned with the hose, Moss threw back his head and strained against the rope.

"Here we go again," Dave warned. "Want to try holding him?"

Zanna clasped Moss around the neck. He was absolutely rigid. With the first squirt of water, he went wild, his jaws snapping, his body contorted. When his soapy head slipped from Zanna's grasp, she felt his mouth on the inside of her arm. It happened so fast and was over so quickly that Zanna didn't even notice that his teeth had broken her skin until Dave said, "You're bleeding. You all right?"

Zanna stared at the puncture marks seeping red. The skin on her arm stung a little, like a scrape. She looked down at Moss, subdued now, standing humped and exhausted.

"He can finish rinsing off in the pond," Dave said. "They can all three go for a swim."

Zanna took Moss's head in her hands. Drenched, the black spots were more prominent on his white face markings. She drew her finger up the narrow blaze between his eyes. "You'll be all right now," she told him.

The moment the dogs were released they dashed uphill and across the road. If a car or truck had been coming, one of them might have been hit, but except for the gleaming tank truck that regularly came to the lower farm to pump out the milk, there was little traffic on Ragged Mountain Road.

Dave hosed off the ramp. He glanced at Zanna. "Better go to the house for something dry. You're a worse mess than I am."

"What about taking the dogs to the pond?"

"I'll do that. Go find Mom or Grandma. Show them the bite."

"No," Zanna objected. "It's not really a bite. He didn't mean to."

"That's not the point. You don't want it infected."

Zanna found Dot and Fennella in the sheep barn separating out some lambs to be sold. There was so much blatting and bawling that Zanna had to shout to be heard over the animals. A good time to tell about her arm, since no one was likely to hear very much.

But Fennella heaved herself over a partition to have a look. "That could stand a bit of cleaning up," she observed as she took Zanna's arm. Shouting to Dot that she'd be back in a few minutes, she led Zanna out of the barn.

"You won't tell my mother, will you?" Zanna asked.

"Not if you do," Fennella replied.

"She'll freak out. It's nothing."

"Nothing's nothing," Fennella retorted. "I'm glad you kids had tetanus shots when you moved up here."

Once they were in the kitchen and Fennella had washed off the arm, Zanna tried again. "Is it all right if Mom doesn't know right away? I mean, before Moss comes."

"You're a stubborn cuss," Fennella remarked, spraying the tooth marks with iodine. "No wonder you're getting somewhere with that dog. That's all. End of sting. I'll just cover it to keep it clean. You'll be fine."

"Will you tell my mother that?" Zanna pleaded.

"I'll get you one of Laurie's shirts to wear," Fennella said noncommittally. "Then take Moss to show Rob how prettied up he is before you bring him home."

Just back from the pond, Moss and Meg were romping together. Even old Queen took a few dives at them before settling down to lick herself in the sun.

Moss was all fluffed out and shiny. He trotted after Zanna to the porch, where Rob sat in his wheelchair. Moss all but climbed into Rob's lap.

"He's still wet," Zanna warned. "He just had a bath. He hated it." Then she added, "He bit me, but I don't think he knows it."

Rob nodded. "Some, some," he said. *Moss, Moss.* He spoke again.

Zanna studied his face, trying to gain meaning from his expression as well as from the garbled words. Reaching over, she raised his hand and placed it on the dog's smooth, shiny head. "He wouldn't hurt anyone on purpose," Zanna insisted. "Except maybe a sheep. Sometimes I think he'd like to teach one a lesson."

Rob smiled with half of his mouth.

On her way back to the sheep barn Fennella called out, "Go on home now and get changed. We'll see you tomorrow."

But Zanna hated taking Moss out from under Rob's lifeless hand. Holding back a moment, she thought she detected something different. Rob's fingers looked as if they were molded to Moss's head. There was a kind of tremor in them, too.

Had Moss felt that small difference? He leaned at an odd angle that couldn't be comfortable. Still, he remained that way, as if he feared to disrupt the light, quivering pressure that came to him from Rob's hand.

When at last Zanna lifted the hand, it seemed to her that she held the shape of the dog's head in the pulsing curve of Rob's fingers.

11

Zanna tied Moss to the porch rail and then went indoors to change. She pulled on a long-sleeved shirt to cover her bandaged arm. After that she felt ready to make a proper entrance with Moss.

Mom was impressed. His black coat shone. The white tail tip and collar were truly white, and so were the lower legs, except where black spots encroached. Zanna had to explain that the black smudges on Moss's white muzzle were pigment spots, not mud.

Mom, at her desk, had been writing something. A letter to Dad? Whatever it was, she seemed anxious to get on with it.

Zanna tried to figure out how to tell her about the dog bite. "We bathed all three dogs," she began.

"Um." Mom stopped writing but didn't turn her head.

"Everything got soaked. I got bitten, too. Should I put my stuff in the washing machine? It's really wet."

"Bitten?" Now Mom did look at her.

"Yes. It isn't anything. Fennella took care of it. What about my clothes?"

For a moment Mom seemed to be considering. The bite? The clothes? Or the letter she was writing? "Might as well, yes. I'll be doing a load later on. You sure you're okay?"

Zanna was already on her way. "Sure," she called back over her shoulder.

At the foot of the stairs Moss balked. It occurred to Zanna that at the farm none of the dogs was allowed upstairs. Before Rob's stroke Moss had sometimes come indoors. He must have learned that a flight of stairs inside the house was off limits.

So Zanna told him these stairs were okay. But he still regarded them as an impassable barrier. First she tried coaxing. Then she resorted to force. Grunting with the effort, she dragged his front half onto the first step, the second step, and finally the third step. But when she placed his forepaws on the fourth step, his hindquarters skidded out from under him. He lay stretched along the lower steps as though spread out to dry.

Next she tried rushing to the upper landing and calling to him in her most commanding tone. Moss actually collected himself and started up. But as soon as he felt himself slide, he stiffened and crashed. Zanna praised him for trying. He stood at the bottom, his tail swinging slowly as she encouraged him. Then she slapped her leg and shouted, "Come!" Moss shot forward and up. He skidded as he climbed. In a wild panic he kept on scrambling for a foothold on each next step until he reached the top.

After hugging him, Zanna took him on a tour of the upstairs. "Here's the bathroom. You won't have anything to do with it." Moss took a gingerly step or two inside, inspected the bathtub, and then backed out. "That way goes to Mom's room. Dad's and Mom's. Stay out, unless they invite you." She turned Moss around. "That room with the closed door is Rachel's. It's always closed, so that's how you tell. And here's mine at the end. Yours and mine."

Moss entered warily. When she asked him to jump on her bed, he shot her a look of horror and bewilderment. Then he walked stiffly to the window, where he raised himself on his forepaws to look out.

"You've just been," she reminded him. "You don't need to go again."

Moss remained at the window, making it plain that he knew his own needs better than she did.

Zanna had pictured him snuggling down with her while she read or did homework. Instead she had to tackle the stairs all over again.

Moss looked down and then shrank from the prospect of descending. Zanna was sure that any dog that could scale a tall gate should be able to handle the stairs, but she wasn't able to convince him. His eyes grew large. His tail disappeared between his legs.

Zanna had to rely on gravity to overcome such profound resistance. In front of him and two steps below, she tugged until his forepaws slid down one step. She tugged harder, willing his hindquarters to follow. When they did, he couldn't stop. While Zanna clutched at the banister, Moss hurtled and bounced all the way to the bottom, where momentum propelled him across the hall to the front door.

"Everything all right?" Mom called. "Did something fall?"

Breathless with laughter, yet somehow close to tears, Zanna shouted back that it was only Moss learning to use the stairs.

"If you're going to play that hard," Mom remarked, "you'd better do it outdoors."

By now Zanna was beside Moss, who yearned toward the front door. "He hates it here," Zanna said. "He hates it."

"Give him something to eat. Dogs settle down when they're fed in a new place," Mom told her.

How did Mom know that? It didn't exactly stack up against Janet's insistence that food should never be used to reward a Border Collie. Still, anything was worth a try.

Since there wasn't any dog food in the house yet, Zanna went in search of something else. She found a jar of soup or stew that Dot had brought over when Mom was sick. Zanna poured some of it into a bowl and set it down in front of Moss. He sniffed with interest and then began to nibble, delicately picking out every chunk of meat and potato and then lapping up the broth. What remained were cut-up vegetables. Zanna offered Moss a piece of carrot. He gave it one polite lick before drawing back. Then he walked to the hall and stood facing the closed front door.

So much for food, thought Zanna. So much for settling in. She took Moss up to the hayland above the house. There he could ramble through familiar haunts and explore fresh traces of animals that had passed his way. Zanna stayed out with him until he was loping easily toward her at her first call. Only then did she turn homeward.

Rachel, who had just come in, made a big fuss over Moss. He responded so playfully that Zanna couldn't help feeling a twinge of envy.

"You don't look all that happy," Mom observed as she headed upstairs. "I thought you'd be thrilled to have the dog here."

"I am," Zanna said lamely. "He isn't."

Mom looked down at Moss, who had rolled on his back to let Rachel rub his belly. "He'll adjust," Mom said. "Give him time."

But neither Mom nor Rachel knew how intense and stubborn Moss could be. At least he hadn't been sent away with a stranger. At least he'd get back to the farm all the time, and to Rob. If Rob was beginning to move his fingers now, maybe that would end some of the confusion for the dog, who probably couldn't understand why his master had suddenly stopped working him and speaking to him or even pressing him close.

That night Rachel helped Zanna start Moss up the stairs. With Rachel boosting him from behind and Zanna tugging him upward, the climb went more smoothly than before.

"Now you've done it twice," Zanna informed him. "Now you've learned how." And although she said this as much to reassure herself as to persuade him, he seemed more at ease up on the landing. It hadn't been such a terrible ordeal after all.

But in her room he paced between the window and the bed. When she reached down to him, her arm began to throb. She almost called Mom about it before she realized that would call attention to the bite. She decided she could stand the pain.

Between her own discomfort and Moss's restlessness, Zanna gave up trying to fall asleep like this. She dragged her quilt from the bed. Spooked by the flapping quilt, Moss sprang out of the way. She didn't try to force him close. She just rolled herself in the quilt and lay on the rug.

Pretty soon Moss dropped beside her. Even though her sore arm was wedged between them, she didn't try to move until she felt him relax against her. Slowly, with care for him and for herself, she freed her arm, turned slightly, and let it rest across his shoulder. He gave a long, deep sigh that sounded almost like a groan, but he didn't stiffen or pull away.

He smelled of soap and pond and, very faintly, of the barn. It came to Zanna that this room was forever changed now, and she was changed. And so was Moss.

12 By Thursday Zanna began to get anxious. Diane was coming home with her Friday on the school bus. If Moss kept freaking out about the stairs, Diane would think he was weird.

The only solution was to spend Friday night with Diane in the furniture room. Calling it camping out, Zanna proposed this to her mother, who automatically rejected the idea. Later she reversed herself. If Diane didn't mind sleeping there, Mom supposed there was no harm in it, just so long as they didn't make a mess of things.

How could they, Zanna wondered, when everything was already all jumbled together in one gigantic mess?

As soon as they got home from school, the girls took Moss for a long walk. After that they carried their sleeping bags into the porch room. Diane thought they should borrow one of the dust-covers and make a tent by positioning a few tall pieces of furniture around the bed.

Moss regarded all the shifting of heavy objects as life-threatening. He plastered himself against the closed door until one bookcase had to be angled in his direction to fit through a gap. As soon as he saw it aimed his way, he took a flying leap, touched down on the back of an armchair, and sprang from it onto Zanna's elevated bed.

"Hey!" Diane exclaimed. "Gymnastics!"

"Let's just cool it for a minute," Zanna suggested. "He's not used to . . . crowded rooms."

Diane clambered up to him and threw her arms around his

neck. It didn't take long for him to flop over on his back and begin doing what she called tricks. Zanna figured he was mostly doing what he felt like or already knew, like lying down on command. But Diane had no doubt that she was teaching him to play dead, roll over, and wave.

Moss reveled in her attention. When she quit rubbing his chest and he began to paw at her, she ordered him to wave. "There!" she declared. "He can learn anything. He should be on television."

They pretended he was. Chairs and a sofa were converted into the audience. Diane started out as the master of ceremonies to show Zanna how. Then she switched over to being a world-famous animal trainer. Moss was her star dog.

Through it all he lolled and flopped around as if he were a born circus dog.

Later he became a desert hound. Diane had seen a movie about people who lived in tents and had hunting dogs. When the girls went to bed, Moss kept guard against the leopards that might steal into the campground while the desert people slept. Mom had let them take a bag of popcorn in with them. Moss stood guard over that, too, their sole provision.

In the morning they found the bag in shreds. Diane praised Moss. Obviously he had fed the leopard the popcorn to keep it from eating the people lying helpless in their sleeping bags.

Zanna went along with all this, but she couldn't help feeling that the Moss she knew had vanished into another life.

Things were different when they went over to the farm. Diane, who had seen sheepdog trials at the Coventry Fair, expected Moss to work the sheep around obstacles, through gates and chutes, and into a pen. All Zanna had Moss do was gather and drive the sheep. She meant to keep the session short, but as usual she lost track of time. By the time Moss was working well, Diane was gone from the gate.

Zanna finally found her in the barnyard peeking through the clogged undercarriage of a manure spreader. "I didn't mean to be so long," Zanna said.

Diane held up a warning finger. "I think there are babies. They went under the black chicken."

"Don't reach in there," Zanna told her. "That hen bites."

"Bites?" Diane drew back. "She's not even moving. She might be dead."

"You'll know she's not dead when she pinches you with that beak."

"Zanna!" Dot called from the back door. "Moss knocked over Rob's pee pot."

"I'll get him," Zanna shouted back. She ran around to the front of the house, Diane trailing behind.

Dot was at the front door now. "Here's hot water and detergent," she said, setting a bucket on the porch. "Slosh it all over the spill. And try to remember not to leave Moss loose if Rob's out here."

Zanna dragged Moss out of the way. Looking guilty and baffled, he scuttled down the steps. She asked Diane to hold him. Then, explaining to Rob that she needed to move the wheelchair, she pulled it back from the table, which was spread with cardboard squares with letters boldly printed on them. She tipped the bucket over the wet area. White suds filled cracks and detoured around swollen floorboards. Soon the porch floor looked like a map.

Dot, at the door again, thrust a broom at Zanna, who swept the map of suds under the porch railing and onto the iris bed below. Moss lurched and broke free, ignoring Diane when she called him to her.

"Moss, lie down!" Zanna ordered. As soon as he dropped to the ground and Diane had a grip on him again, Zanna set the broom aside. "Moss doesn't like brooms," she said to Rob as she pushed the chair back in place. "He acts like they're after him. He acts like that about a lot of things," she went on. "We need a whole list of what Moss doesn't like."

"Some," said Rob, while Diane stared up from the lawn.

"Moss," Zanna responded.

Rob nodded. "Toom. Chum."

"Tomb?"

"Snow." He shook his head. "Toom chum."

Chum could mean "friend" or "pal." "The girl holding Moss is Diane," she told him. "Diane's my best friend."

"Some," he repeated more forcefully. He was sounding frustrated.

"I'm trying to understand," she said to him. Turning to the cardboard letters on the table, she spelled out *chum*. She glanced at Rob. No, that wasn't it. She knew it was risky spelling out words for him because she was such a bad speller. She moved the *chum* letters around until they turned into *much*.

"Ah," Rob declared, excitement producing a trickle of saliva from the corner of his mouth.

She couldn't decipher *toom* that easily. Or was it *tomb*? But when she put the two words together and she said them out loud, she came up with *too much*.

"So, so," Rob exclaimed. "God," he brought out with effort. "Some."

She stared at the words, stared at him. All of a sudden it came to her. "Too much dog! Moss is too much dog?"

The sobbing she now recognized as laughter was her answer.

"Too much for who?" she asked.

"Fellen," he said. Or was it *felon*? Or *fell in*? Amazingly, he followed this up with "Dot."

That was all the clue Zanna needed. Fellen was Fennella. Rob was saying that Moss was too much dog for Fennella and Dot.

"Sometimes," she admitted, "he's too much for me, too. Only once in a while," she added.

"So, so," Rob agreed. "Some. God doog."

Astonishment welled up in her. This was a real conversation now. It felt like one of her breakthroughs with Moss.

She hated to tear herself away. But Diane was waiting for her.

On the way home Diane was full of questions about Rob, about how much he understood and felt. "Isn't he creepy?" she said.

As they crossed the pasture, Moss scooted off in too wide an arc. Zanna, suspecting he might sneak around behind the sheep, called to him. He loped around in an easy circle and returned to the girls. Diane reached down to ruffle his coat. She told him what a good boy he was. He couldn't have looked more innocent. So Zanna didn't try to explain that he had just been testing her, seeing what he could get away with.

Diane enticed Moss to race her toward the far gate. They looked like the dog and kid Zanna had once pictured, only with herself and Moss—that heartwarming scene right out of a Disney movie.

13

After dropping Diane off at her house, Mom and Zanna stopped at the supermarket to pick up some Saturday specials on sale. Mom said it was to make up for spending too much on prepared foods lately.

Zanna was glad she hadn't told Mom about feeding the frozen dinner to Moss. But she did summon up enough courage to ask about the fancy food Dad had brought home with him on his last visit. Zanna hoped Mom's answer would hold a clue to her feelings for Dad.

But Mom only said, "Thrift doesn't come easily to your father. Besides—" She broke off. Zanna waited. "It was special, like a party."

"Didn't you want it?" Zanna asked her.

"I guess it makes me . . . uncomfortable when I'm trying hard to save."

Her stumbling explanation didn't clarify anything Zanna longed to know. Neither of them spoke again for a while, until Zanna broke the silence by asking Mom how she managed to unscramble so many of Rob's words.

As Mom drove out of town, she mentioned training and experience. And then she opened up some more. She thought Rob was getting easier to understand. She thought that his improved mobility went along with his improved speech.

"I got a whole sentence today," Zanna told her.

"He spoke it correctly, or you guessed it?"

"He got one word right. I figured out the others."

Mom reminded her how important it was to keep Rob trying for the correct words. "Everyone in his family caves in as soon as he gets irritable," she added.

"What do you do?" Zanna asked.

"I let him get mad. I tell him I'll do my best if he does his. The other day, though, I was the one who fouled up. I tried to get him to unscramble some nonsense phrase. Luckily Fennella overheard us and straightened me out. It was a dog command."

"Which one?" Zanna wanted to know.

Mom shook her head. "Something that contradicted itself. Oh, yes. 'Away to me.' That was it. I thought it couldn't be 'away' and 'to me' at the same time."

"So what happened?" Zanna asked her.

"Nothing. I apologized, and Rob had a good laugh."

"How long will he go on having therapy?" Zanna said.

Mom glanced at her for a second and then concentrated on

her driving. "You mean, when will we have to leave Ragged Mountain Farm? I don't know. And it's not just about therapy and the free house. I don't even know where we'll be when school starts next year."

"You mean you might lose your job, too?"

Mom shook her head. "I mean we may be moving west. It depends."

Depends on what? Zanna wanted to demand. But she could tell that Mom was edging away from any further revelation. Backing off, Zanna asked why it was harder to get work in New England than other parts of the country.

"It's complicated." Mom sighed. "It's economics."

That meant she didn't want to go into that subject either.

They turned onto Ragged Mountain Road. Zanna understood that Mom had been telling her not to count on its being home much longer. But Zanna didn't think any other place could ever be more home than this.

She looked out at the steep fields dropping away from the dirt road, the stands of trees that lined the fences. She looked the other way toward the dense woodlots pressing down from the upper reaches of the mountain. Home. And Moss tied to the porch, standing as they drove to the house that didn't belong to them. Mom wanted Zanna to keep in mind that this was Laurie's house still, Laurie's and Dave's, Dot's and Gordon's. None of it could last, no matter what happened.

Carrying grocery bags past the tied dog proved tricky. Moss tried too hard to get out of the way and managed to get his rope underfoot, however he dodged. By the time the car was unloaded Mom was out of sorts. She told Zanna to take the dog for a walk. Not Moss. The dog. She always seemed to forget his name when she was in a bad mood.

Zanna retreated with Moss to the furniture room. Without Diane it was just a bunch of shapes and lumps under dustcovers.

But Moss jumped onto Zanna's real bed without being asked. Circling, he grunted twice and curled up tight. When she clambered up beside him, he gave a nervous growl. But he didn't jump down.

Zanna tried to restore her old arrangement, with some of her books and a pad and pencils and markers within arm's reach. There were also a few socks, one of them Diane's. And scraps from the popcorn bag. She neatened up by stuffing the scraps into a sock.

Then she went to work with the pad and pencil. She started listing the words she knew, like *some* and *doog* and *god* and *toom* and *chum* and *silo*. Next she started a list of words she hadn't figured out. It didn't matter how she spelled them. They couldn't be more wrong than when Rob spoke them.

If only homework produced puzzles like this, she'd ace all her assignments. Well, maybe not ace them. After all, the words remained a mystery. But they were a challenge, and there was a purpose in solving them. Think what it would mean for Rob to find his way through them to being understood. Think what that would mean to everyone in his life. It would certainly put an end to any secret plan to sell Moss to Mr. Nearing.

PART THREE

1 Long after the fields and pastures came to life, winter clung to the summit of Ragged Mountain. During Zanna's afternoon rambles with Moss, she was never sure whether a distant whiteness among the upland trees came from a drift of blossoms, shad or wild apple, or from a trace of snow untouched by the sun.

Then the last ice jams broke. Streams tumbled downhill, and the woods were boisterous with birds that sounded like cows and tree frogs that sounded like birds. Down around the farm the last of the lambs and ewes put out to graze shrilled back and forth, losing and finding each other over and over and setting the calves to bawling.

These days there was usually the drone of a tractor in fields where Gordon or Dot were harrowing and planting. Everyone at the farm was occupied during every daylight minute, including Dave from the moment he got home from school.

Only Rob sat still.

Zanna brought Moss to him every day. Now that lambs were out with the ewes, Zanna had to make sure that Moss didn't push them too hard. "Keep a lid on the dog" was the way Fennella put it.

One day when Dot had to run over to Janet's place, she took Zanna and Moss along. Janet had wanted them to get the feel of different sheep on new ground. The newness excited Moss. By the time he settled down, his tongue was hanging out of the side of his mouth and he was ready to flop.

"Don't let the dog in the sheep water," Janet's older boy, Steven, told Zanna when it was already too late. There was Moss in the tub, with only his head showing, his ears floating on the surface. "Now you have to change the water," Steven informed her.

Zanna called Moss out of the tub. "How does your mother change the water?" she asked Steven.

"With the hose," he said.

She went looking for a hose and found only the heavy-duty kind attached to pipes between rows of tiny trees.

"Dad doesn't let dogs near his nursery trees," Steven told her.

"Moss!" she shouted before realizing that Moss was up by the house. "Good boy," she said when he cast her a questioning look. He hadn't done anything wrong. She was the one who was out of her depth.

She turned to ask Steven where to find a hose, but he and his little brother, Tim, had vanished. Dot and Janet were talking with Rick, Janet's husband, down behind the stand. So Zanna looked in a shed that was full of equipment and bales of peat moss. When she came out, the two little boys met her. They were sharing a box of Froot Loops.

"Are you taking care of us?" Steven asked her.

That brought Zanna up short. Was she supposed to be watching them? And where was Moss now? She called him and called again, her voice rising with alarm. She had yelled at him when he was nowhere near the baby trees, and now he had gone off.

She was about to run to the stand for help when Dot and Janet drove up to the house in Janet's van and hauled something out of the back. Dot went into the house, but Janet stopped to ask Zanna how Moss had done with the sheep.

"The dog went in the water," Steven told her.

"I couldn't find a hose," Zanna started to explain. "I don't know where Moss is."

"I'll take care of the water later," Janet said.

The door of the house opened, and Moss shot out.

"How did he get in the house?" Zanna exclaimed.

"We had him cleaning up something," Steven said. He

crammed a fistful of Froot Loops into his mouth and gazed at her in wide-eyed innocence.

Zanna choked back a retort. He had known perfectly well where Moss was and had let her stew over him for nothing.

The next thing Zanna knew, Janet was thanking her for keeping the boys entertained. She proposed bringing Zanna to a sheepdog trial in exchange for helping again with the boys.

Was anything, even a sheepdog trial, worth having to put up with ghastly Steven and his little brother?

Janet went on to explain that the trial would be held on a large farm. Zanna could learn a lot watching dogs run sheep in its big field. Besides, it would be good for Moss to get used to all the commotion.

"But he's been in trials," Zanna said, thinking of the tray Moss had won.

Janet nodded. "That was last season. And Grampa was in charge. It's a whole new ball game this year. You up for it?"

Zanna hesitated. If Moss got wound up just coming to Janet's, how would he behave at the sheepdog trial? Then, of course, there was Steven to contend with. But Zanna couldn't resist the invitation. She told Janet she would go.

Once the plan was made, Zanna could hardly wait. She was to spend Saturday night at Janet's because they had to get such an early start the next morning. And that would give her a chance to get Moss out on Janet's sheep again.

And then what? If this trial day worked out well for Janet, there would be more to come. And sooner or later, when Moss seemed ready, Zanna might even get to run him herself.

2 The little boys were still asleep in the back of the van when Janet drove into the parking area. People greeted her as she got out. Almost every camper and car, truck and motor home had dogs attached. There was no barking, no growling.

The trial course was set out in a vast field that dipped down in the center and then rose gradually to a ridge at the top end. The fetch gate in the middle looked a mile away. The drive gates were placed way off to each side of the field. Zanna couldn't imagine Moss driving such distances.

Janet introduced her to a woman named Beezie and then told her to walk Moss around on a leash to get him used to being near so many strange dogs. The little boys woke up crabby and hungry. Janet took care of them and then brought them over to the fence to watch the first runs with Zanna.

Someone at the far end of the field used a dog to bring four sheep out of a holding pen and settled them beside a stake on the ridge. Each competing handler stood beside another stake a short distance from the spectators lining the fence and sent the competing dog up the field to gather the four sheep. The judge watched every move and spoke to a clerk, who wrote down the scores for every phase of the dog's work.

It was different watching this trial, not just because the course was so much bigger than at the Coventry Fair but because now Zanna could recognize good work and even, sometimes, bad handling. Most of the handlers whistled their commands, only resorting to spoken words now and then.

When it was time for Janet to get ready to run Tess, she put Zanna in charge of the little boys. Luckily they had just found some friends and were allowed to play with them in their motor home.

Now that more spectators were arriving, an announcer on a public-address system told them what to look for. "The handler is waiting for the sheep to settle," he said. "Okay. There goes the dog. To the right. Time is up eleven minutes after the handler sends the dog."

When Janet's turn came and Tess brought the sheep down the field, Zanna could feel Moss shudder with excitement. Zanna found herself listening as much to the other handlers' comments as to the announcer. "Nice gather," Beezie commented. "Good line on the drive," someone else remarked. The announcer seemed to agree. He pronounced it a first-class run, even though Tess had had trouble shedding one sheep off from the group and holding it away from the others. Zanna wondered whether Tess had a chance of placing among the top ten dogs that would compete for final points after all the dogs had run once. Beezie said it was too early to tell.

A man who said he was the trial manager tapped Zanna on the shoulder. Would she like to help out at the exhaust pen? Janet had said it was all right as long as her boys were getting along with the other kids. Janet would be taking Tess up on the ridge to set out sheep for the next few runs.

Zanna nodded. Before she had to admit that she had no idea what an exhaust pen was, the trial manager showed her where Janet and Tess had just put the sheep they had worked. It didn't mean a pen for exhausted sheep or even tired ones; it was just a place to put those that had been used. Zanna was supposed to stand inside the pen with Moss until each run was completed and then, and only then, open the gate and send Moss to pen the four used sheep.

As soon as the next handler cast his dog out to gather a new group of four sheep, Moss climbed partway up the gate to watch. When the sheep and dog drew near, he began to whimper.

"Keep that dog quiet," ordered a man in a tone so nasty that Zanna jerked Moss down from the gate and hurled herself on top of him.

"Don't let him get to you," another handler remarked. "He's just bent out of shape because he messed up his first dog's run."

Zanna clamped Moss's muzzle in her hands. She was so intent on silencing him that she lost track of the run and wasn't ready with Moss when it was over.

"Open the gate now," the kind handler instructed. "Send your dog on a come bye. That's the way."

Moss flew wide to the left.

"Call him in, call him in," the handler told her. "That's it. Now lie him down. Slow the sheep."

"Thank you," she said to him after she had dragged the gate shut. But he was off to get his own dog, and the next time she saw him he was walking out to the starting post with his left hand slightly raised to place his dog in quiet readiness for the outrun. She was glad to see him handle his dog so well. It seemed right that someone who took time to help a kid like her would have a good clean run of his own.

Soon she and Moss got into the routine of fetching in the used sheep. She kept watching for the nasty man's next run. Then she nearly forgot about him because there were two disastrous runs, one right after the other. In each instance the sheep split. One handler quit because he couldn't get his dog to put them back together. The other dog was disqualified by the judge.

Zanna had to send Moss all the way up the field to gather each group of sheep. He was in his element on these deep outruns, each time swinging wide and putting the scattered sheep back together before bringing them in a bit too fast but straight to her.

"I told them they should put Moss to work." The voice came from just outside the fence. She wheeled around. Mr. Nearing stood there, looking pleased and proud, as though he were responsible for Moss's performance.

Zanna didn't know what to say to him. She was facing him, not looking at Moss, when the next dog was cast off to gather four new sheep. She didn't see Moss spring up and over the gate until he was on his way up the field, determined to reach those sheep before the other outrunning dog stole them away.

"Moss, no!" she shrieked. "Lie down, Moss! Lie down!"

But there was no stopping him now. She was so mortified that she didn't even notice the judge stepping over to the handler at the stake and telling him to recall his dog. She did see the dog turn back, though. She could also tell that Janet, on the ridge, had brought Moss back under control.

The judge called to Zanna to bring the sheep to the exhaust pen. So Zanna had to stand in front of the entire audience while Moss fetched the wasted sheep down the field.

When it was over and the sheep were penned, she saw the manager approach. The nasty handler was with him, demanding that the kid with the unmanageable dog be removed from the trial course. Only then did she realize that he had been the handler at the post. Those were his sheep that Moss had stolen.

The manager agreed that Zanna would be replaced at the exhaust pen before the nasty handler had his rerun. Meanwhile, Zanna should keep Moss leashed while the competing dogs were on the course.

Zanna would have preferred to hide in the van, where no one would see her or Moss. Even after everything was going as smoothly as before her major mess, her face still burned.

At last the announcer declared a half hour break for lunch. The two little boys appeared across the fence from Zanna. They were hungry.

Zanna was actually glad to see them. Someone shouted to her to let all the sheep out of the exhaust pen to graze. Then she joined the boys. First Steven had to go to the portable john. Beezie held Moss and Tim so that Zanna could take care of Steven.

"Moss looked good out there," Beezie remarked as she handed Tim back to Zanna.

"He was awful," Zanna blurted. "He spoiled that man's run."

Beezie shrugged. "Want to know something? That man, Billy Mount, is on top of the world."

Zanna gaped at her.

Janet, arriving just then, picked up on this. "Beezie's right. Moss did Billy a big favor. His dog will get to rerun at the very end of the trial, when the sheep will have gone over the course at least once."

"I'm hungry," Steven reminded everyone.

"Sandwiches in the van," Janet told him. Turning to Zanna, she asked how Moss had gotten away like that.

"Mr. Nearing came over," Zanna answered. "He was talking to me. I wasn't paying attention to Moss."

Janet nodded. "And Moss was all steamed up after those two big gathers. Well," she added, "I guess you'll never let Howard Nearing distract you again." She grinned. "Not a bad lesson for your first trial."

And that was all she said about it.

3 During the midday break people stopped by to ask about Rob. Many of them said it didn't feel right starting the new trial season without him. A few asked what was going to happen to Moss. "That promising young dog" was the way one of them put it. When someone expressed surprise that he was put in the hands of a kid, Janet just smiled at Zanna and remarked that they should see Moss when a grown man like her father tried to work him.

After lunch Zanna took the little boys and their friends frogging along a nearby stream. While they splashed around and got muddy, the whistles and shouts that came from the trial field tugged at Zanna. Still, it was a relief not having to think about every move she and Moss made.

By midafternoon the children were finished with frogs and mud. After Zanna managed to get all the right shoes and socks back on, she took the children to the van for cookies. Then they all went off to find their parents.

Zanna was just in time to watch Billy Mount's rerun. She hoped he would fall on his face. She hoped he would be so rattled that he would forget which way to drive the sheep. She hoped he behaved so badly that the judge disqualified him for poor sportsmanship.

When Billy Mount walked to the stake with his dog, a hush fell over the audience. The dog took off like a shot. Too close? Too tight? It looked that way to Zanna, whose spiteful heart soared at the prospect of Billy Mount's humiliation. Only now the dog was widening out. "There's your pear-shaped outrun," the announcer informed the spectators. "That's the ideal we all aim for." Even without his reverent commentary, Zanna could see for herself that both handler and dog were in perfect command. When the score was posted, it merely confirmed the obvious: This was the best run of the day so far.

By now the two little boys were growing restless. They seemed to sense the exact instant Janet's attention left them. She needed time to collect her thoughts before her final run with Tess.

Zanna lured the boys away from Janet with the promise of

more dessert. She took them to a table where a local church group was selling homemade cakes, only to find that she didn't have enough money.

"Let me help you." Mr. Nearing was beside her. He forked over a wad of bills to the woman behind the table. "Four," he said. "Coffee for me. They'll tell you what they want for drinks."

"Oh, that's all right," Zanna protested. "I couldn't—"

"It's nothing," he told her.

"I'll get the money after—"

"My treat," he said expansively. He leaned over to pat Moss on the head and said to the dog, "Sorry I can't do the same for you, boy."

"Well, thank you," Zanna said lamely. She had to stifle an impulse to yank Moss out of Mr. Nearing's reach.

She got the boys back to the fence just as the announcer explained that the top ten dogs' first and second scores would be combined to determine final placings. Zanna tried to listen to all the explanations, keep an eye on the boys, who were making more of a mess with frosting than they had with frogs and mud, and still watch the runs.

When Janet and Tess walked to the post, Zanna could tell by Janet's stillness how utterly she was focused on the sheep and dog. Tim squeezed in front of Zanna, stared through the fence, and then thrust one chocolate-smeared fist toward his mother. "Mommee! Mommee, look!" he bellowed.

Drawing him against her, Zanna clapped her hand over his mouth. "Mommy's looking at the sheep," she whispered to him. "Can you see them, too?"

Shoving her hand aside, he boomed, "Where?"

"Ssh. There." Zanna pointed. She managed to keep him quiet by issuing her own running commentary. It had little resemblance to the announcer's, and it made it almost impossible for her to follow Tess's run. "Pretty soon it will be time to clap your hands," she told the child. "Ready?" She held his hands apart, poised.

"Now?" he demanded in his deep voice.

"Ssh. Nearly. You watch." If he clapped while Tess was about to shed off one sheep, it could startle the animals and spoil the shed.

The four sheep lined up. They streamed off in the direction of the exhaust pen. Just before they left the shedding ring, Janet called Tess through and turned the last sheep away.

The spectators cheered and clapped. Tim burst into tears.

"You said I could clap," he wailed.

"Well, you can," Zanna told him. "Go ahead now."

But he shook his head and sobbed that the other people had taken his turn. All Zanna could do was hold him against her and let him cry.

That was how Janet found them. Steven demanded to know whether Janet had just won the trial. Tim insisted on his mother's undivided attention while he clapped for her.

Janet held him while she and Zanna watched the rest of the final runs. When they were over, most of the handlers had a fairly good idea of the trial's outcome. A woman named Beverly had knocked Billy Mount out of first place, but he held on to second. Janet moved up one notch, finishing sixth.

The trial manager showed up to ask Zanna if she would like to fetch the sheep down from the ridge and put them with the others in the exhaust pen. They had to be moved across the road as soon as the awards were given out.

Zanna and Moss darted through the milling spectators and handlers, most of them heading for the tent with the trophies and ribbons and envelopes containing money. She made him walk beside her the way she had seen the handlers and their dogs start their runs. She even stopped him at the post and surveyed the sheep released from the holding pen and already spread out on the ridge. Then she sent Moss to gather them.

His outrun was probably wider than the judge would have liked to see, but the judge wasn't watching. No one was. Zanna couldn't resist trying to bring the sheep through the fetch gates. As they moved down the field, Zanna realized they were coming too fast. She flanked Moss to the left and then way over to the right to crowd them through. After that she let him continue, with the sheep gathering speed. She had to race ahead to open the gate before they reached the exhaust pen.

She felt like whooping with glee. How did Janet or any of the other good handlers keep from jumping for joy when things went so well?

"Nice work," someone remarked to her as she hurried over to the crowd at the tent. So she had been seen after all. She was glad she hadn't done anything stupid out there.

She noticed Mr. Nearing slipping off to his car. Why did this give her such an uneasy feeling? He wasn't hanging around for the awards. Yet he had stayed this long. To watch Moss working again? Why did he keep following her and Moss around? What was in it for him?

4 Zanna arrived home bursting with all she wanted to tell about her day. She walked in on a conversation between Mom and Rachel.

"How near will we be to Hollywood?" Rachel was asking.

Hollywood?

"Nothing's settled yet," Mom answered guardedly. "There's lots to be worked out before we move." And then, almost under her breath, she added, "If we move."

Zanna tried to take all of this in. Moss trotted into the kitchen. She could hear him lapping water from his bowl.

"We've always been going to go as soon as Dad got permanently hired," Rachel blurted. "So what do you mean, *if*?"

"I'm not sure. It's the timing . . ." Mom's words fell away. Only then did she turn to Zanna to inform her that Dad had called with the momentous news that he had been hired full-time.

Zanna felt as if she were floating somewhere above them and hearing all this from a distance. Then Moss thrust his wet muzzle into her hand, and she dropped down from space. Sinking to her knees, she hugged him hard. She couldn't think of anything to say because the question she needed to ask was about him, and she was afraid of the answer she might hear.

She took Moss to visit Rob, who was in the parlor, his wheelchair pushed up to a card table. He half leaned on it, his left hand fumbling toward a mug.

"We're back from the sheepdog trial," she announced as she came around to face him. "Janet was sixth."

Rob used his fingers to push himself back. They worked like crooked props, helping him to shift the balance of his body. Only then could he meet her eyes. "Bring home . . . ?"

She studied his expression, her mind scrambling to assemble clues to those two words. She could see that he was teasing and eager all at the same time.

"I brought home Moss," she told him.

"Ah." Rob's wrist rotated slightly. He was offering his hand to the dog. Moss sat close, his chin resting on the upturned palm.

Zanna told Rob all about the day, trying to remember as many names as she could. When she told about Moss taking off after Billy Mount's sheep, Rob threw back his head and laughed a real laugh. Only as it ended was the sound drawn out in a kind of sob.

"And I sent Moss all the way up the field to bring the last sheep down at the end of the trial," she finished. "Straight through the fetch gates. It wasn't by accident. I tried. Someone said how good he looked. Someone—" She broke off. She would not mention Mr. Nearing. "Everyone said they missed you."

Fennella came in with a mug of tea. "Janet was in a hurry," she said to Rob. "You were napping when she dropped Zanna off. She said she'd be back later to fill you in on all the trial gossip."

Rob sighed. His upper body strained to raise itself from its slumped position. Fennella pulled him up in the chair. She turned to Zanna. "I hear there's big changes afoot in your family."

"I don't know much about it," Zanna mumbled.

She waited for Fennella to say something about Moss. But all she said was "I guess no one does. Your mother wants Rob to go for a full evaluation while she's still around for follow-up work. Then she'll lay out a program for after she's gone." Fennella shook her head. "It'll be strange carrying on without her."

Zanna watched Rob lean over his mug and sip the tea through a straw. How did he feel about losing Mom? She had been giving him therapy through all these months.

"I wish we could stay," Zanna blurted. "I love it here."

Fennella regarded her as she helped Rob straighten up from his mug. "I bet you'll love California, too. And you'll have your dad again."

Zanna nodded. If only she could ask about Moss.

"Anyway"—Fennella went on—"if Rob keeps on improving like this, the time will come when Dot and Gordon and the kids can move back into their own house."

Zanna nodded again. She didn't need to be reminded that this entire arrangement was temporary.

Back home Zanna visited the furniture room. For the first time her private space there failed to call to her. One day soon all these things would be loaded in a van and unpacked in another house. Near Hollywood? Rachel had sounded thrilled at the prospect. Even though she had landed only a small part in the school play, it had changed her life. Her future was in acting. She was sure of it.

Yet beneath all the excitement Rachel was worried. About what she had called the trial separation? About Mom's reservations? Zanna couldn't tell.

That night she lay in bed and tried to imagine what it would be like if her parents really did split. Would she be asked to choose between them like that girl in Rachel's class? How would she ever be able to inform her own mother and father that she loved a dog more than anything else in the whole wide world?

At school she told Diane about what seemed to be in the works.

Diane kept shaking her head. "You've been my best friend since second grade."

"I know," Zanna answered. "Me, too. I don't want to move."

"Not even to California?"

"If we go, what will happen to Moss?"

"Oh." Diane considered. "Why don't you ask them?"

But Zanna couldn't bring herself to put her worst fears into words, not even to Diane. "He might end up back in the cow barn on a chain" was all she could manage. The other possibility—that he might, after all, be sold to Mr. Nearing for thousands of dollars—stuck in her throat.

5 School had been out two weeks when Dad came home for a long weekend. He was in high spirits the whole time; Mom was subdued. There were no arguments, only long conversations with their door closed or long walks by themselves.

"They must be working it out," Rachel said to Zanna.

But Zanna couldn't help wondering whether Rachel had dreamed up the whole separation idea in the first place.

The plans taking shape emerged in fragments, like puzzle pieces long missing. Mom's job was a major stumbling block. She would not leave until she had seen certain projects through or safely passed on to someone competent to take over.

By the end of the weekend it was decided that she would fly out west to house-hunt and to explore job possibilities.

Still no one mentioned Moss.

The summer routine was established. Rachel and Laurie worked afternoons at Janet and Rick's stand. Zanna sat for the boys three times a week, worked Moss, and spent time with Rob when everyone else was either haying or working at the stand. She would move him out of the sun and would bring him a snack or a drink. She emptied his urinal now, too. It was simply part of the whole scene, which included sitting across from him with the Scrabble board between them, playing games that no one else would have tolerated.

It didn't matter how badly Zanna spelled, not in front of Rob. Occasionally he poked a crooked finger at one of her letters and nudged it off its square. She only shrugged and offered another spelling, if one occurred to her. Sometimes they ended up laughing over her creative lettering the way they did over his misnamed words. What a pair they were, each of them losers, with no one around to correct them.

When it wasn't too hot, Zanna took Moss walking, just to be alone with him in their favorite haunts. The only place she couldn't bring herself to return to was the field where he had first run from her. The pain of losing him, or of thinking she had, was stronger than her memory of his coming back to her of his own accord.

Sometimes she found a note on the farm kitchen table asking her to bring cold drinks out to Dot and Gordon and Dave and Fennella in the heat of the day. Other times, when the hay wagons came in, she helped pass along the bales that tipped off the elevator.

As long as the big round bales were left on the fields, Zanna used them as obstacles for working sheep. By now she felt safe letting Moss bring a few ewes across the road to the obstacle course.

Rob watched from the porch when he could. He even offered a suggestion now and again. "Wider," he might say. "Slow." Not *silo* anymore, but *slow*.

"That's hard," she would answer. "Moss doesn't like slow."

And Rob would send her a look that was perfectly clear: Who's in charge, you or the dog?

It was such good practicing ground that Janet came some early mornings to work Tess there, too. But then along came the tractor with the forklift to pick up the bales and clear the field so that a second hay crop would grow.

Janet took Zanna to a few more sheepdog trials, precious days away from the unending work on both the farm and the nursery.

The first trial was disappointing. Zanna had to keep a sharp eye on the little boys because the course was beside a busy road.

No one invited her and Moss to exhaust sheep. It was probably just as well. Moss was edgy that day. When an early-afternoon thunderstorm hit, Zanna guessed that he must have felt it coming. She had her hands full holding on to him while she kept the boys under cover.

The second trial started with novice classes. Since Moss had already placed in open trials, Zanna was allowed to run him only in the most advanced novice class. That meant competing with real handlers and their young dogs. She felt shy about entering Moss until she found out that there were other beginners and even two kids.

At the last minute Janet decided to leave the boys with Laurie and Rachel. The change of plans made Janet and Zanna late for the trial. As soon as they arrived, it was time for Moss to run. The judge took a moment to explain the course to Zanna. When she walked with Moss to the starting post, her heart pounding, her ears buzzing, he danced beside her, aching to be off. She tried to calm him, but her mouth was so dry that all that came out of it was a kind of croak.

"Wait for the sheep to settle," the judge advised.

As she turned to thank the judge, Moss bounded forward. She had to call him back to her side. She could hear him panting with excitement. If only she had had time to let him unwind before coming to the course. If only she had been able to watch some of the runs ahead of her.

"The sheep are waiting," the judge pointed out.

She cast off Moss to the right because the sheep might try to bolt for the holding pen in the upper right corner of the field. The moment she sent him, she could tell that he wanted to run left; he was too tight. She was afraid to shout at him to get back out. If he thought she was angry, that would only make matters worse. When he swung around behind the sheep, he still looked close. But to her surprise, the sheep didn't stir. He walked toward them. Slowly they turned and started down the field toward her. Zanna began to breathe more easily.

But the lead sheep kept bearing off to the side. Zanna called, or tried to call, to Moss to flank hard, but again all that she could utter was a squawk. Still, either Moss heard her or else took over on his own. He veered out to head the rogue sheep. For a moment the little flock angled sharply. Zanna shouted at Moss to lie down. He froze. The sheep slowed. Zanna was so rattled she had to turn her whole body and face the same way as Moss to figure out how to direct him.

"Away to me!" she called to him.

Moss obeyed, coming in above the sheep and setting them straight again. As they scurried through the fetch gates, Zanna wondered whether she ought to quit now while Moss still looked good. Then again, maybe she was running out of time. If she just held on a little longer, it would probably all be over.

Now the sheep were on their way to the first drive gates. They were going through. At least that was how it looked to Zanna, who swung Moss to the left to make a nice clean turn. To her dismay she saw that Moss had turned the sheep a second too soon. Two of them slipped just in front of the inside panel, failing to go through.

Zanna was so disappointed that she simply shut down. It was Moss who kept going, Moss whose steady crossdrive brought her back to the job at hand. She collected herself in time to see that the sheep were sloping away from the next gates. Because she couldn't think of what to tell Moss, she shouted to him to lie down. Luckily he disobeyed her and took control of the runaway sheep.

Then everything happened too fast. Zanna raced to the pen but couldn't open the gate in time for the oncoming sheep. They pressed against the side of the pen, where they didn't belong.

"Moss," she whispered, "get back out."

Moss crept backward and to the side. Not enough.

"Out," she repeated softly so as not to spook the sheep. As he slunk away, the sheep edged toward the opening, trickling one at a time, slowly, like honey dripping from a spoon. She slammed the gate shut.

It was Beezie who brought the news that Moss had placed fifth in his class. Fifth!

"Grampa will be tickled," Janet said.

"But how could he be fifth?" Zanna blurted. "We messed up so much. *I* messed up."

"Obviously," Janet answered with a laugh, "the others must have messed up even worse. It's probably a good thing you weren't around to see their runs. You would have been a nervous wreck."

Would have been? thought Zanna. It had been the scariest thing she had ever tried to do. And yet she was ready to do it all over again. She would have given anything for another chance. Reaching down to Moss, she felt the thrust of his muzzle against her hand.

"Now what's wrong with this dog's outrun?" Janet asked as they stood watching the beginning of the open trial.

Zanna turned her attention to the dog running along the inside of the fence. "Out of contact with the sheep?"

"Maybe," Janet said. "Anyway, losing valuable time and energy."

Time, thought Zanna, was something else when you stood at the post. She was sure she had been out there with Moss for at least an hour. She tried to recall his outrun, but it was a blur. Anyway, there were other dogs to watch now and learn from. Somehow she had to wipe the silly grin off her face and act as though placing fifth was all in a day's work.

6

When Rob didn't respond to Zanna's account of the trial, when he took no notice of Moss's ribbon, his aloof manner forced her to try even harder to impress him. But nothing she said worked.

Later she asked her mother what was going on. Mom talked about Rob's upcoming evaluation. Only how did that explain his remoteness?

"Janet said he'd be tickled over Moss placing fifth," Zanna told her mother. "But he wasn't. He wasn't proud of Moss." As she spoke, she heard her own voice again. Had Rob detected in it a shift away from Moss toward her own triumph?

Mom supposed Rob was anxious about going away from home. The rehabilitation clinic was a lot farther than the hospital. Zanna didn't see how that would make him lose interest in Moss, though. Was something else going on?

The next morning Zanna tried to get Rachel to talk about it. But Rachel was all wrapped up in her grief at having to leave Dave. Since she was spending what little free time he had with him, Laurie began to come over and hang out with Zanna.

A few days after the trial Laurie talked about the changes that would have to be made at the farm so that Fennella could manage Rob by herself. A downstairs toilet was a must. If they could afford it, a whole bathroom. They wouldn't know how much they had to spend until the evaluation was done and they learned whether it made sense to get Rob a power wheelchair.

"Are they—" Zanna swallowed. "Is anyone still talking about selling Moss?"

Laurie turned away. "Uh-huh."

Zanna wasn't sure whether that meant yes or no. "What are they saying?" she insisted.

Laurie shook her head. "I'm not supposed to talk about it."

So they were. "Does Rob know?" Zanna asked.

Laurie whipped around. "Of course not. And you're not supposed to either. If you say a word to anyone, I'm in big trouble."

"How much?" Zanna whispered.

"I don't know. Plenty. Oh, you mean, how much for Moss?" Laurie shrugged again. "I'm not sure. Mr. Nearing offered three thousand. Dad's holding out for more."

"But Moss isn't his to sell," Zanna protested. "How can he do it?"

"I guess Grandma's changing her mind. Because of all the stuff she needs for Grampa. Besides, after you go, Moss will be back at the farm again. Dad thinks we should unload him right now while he's going good for you."

Zanna wanted to scream and cry, to accuse all the Catherwoods of being greedy and heartless. She managed to keep that rage inside. She managed to ask Laurie how come Fennella changed her mind when she knew what Moss meant to Rob.

"Well," Laurie responded, "she can see that Grampa's used to Moss being here with you. So maybe he won't mind too much if Mr. Nearing buys him. Considering," she added.

"Considering what?" Zanna demanded.

"I don't know. Mr. Nearing can't finish the training by himself. So there might be a deal with Janet. That way Moss would be around some."

"That isn't like having him here!" Zanna exploded. "Rob sees him practically every day. And what about Moss? Doesn't anyone care about him?"

"Oh, get real," Laurie snapped. "They're just trying to figure things out. Nothing's decided. If Grandma had her way, and Janet, too, Janet would just take Moss. But how can they pay for everything they need? The power wheelchair by itself is thousands."

Zanna could feel herself choking up. How could Fennella betray Rob? How could Janet go on coaching Zanna and Moss as if they had a future?

"Do me a favor," Laurie was saying, "keep this to yourself. They didn't want you all bent out of shape over Moss."

Sure, thought Zanna. All this time she worked so hard wasn't for the dog. It was so that he would bring in more money when it was time to sell him.

She took off with Moss. Through the hayland above the house. Laurie's house. And beyond the fields to the woods. The day was still, even the insects silent, only occasional creaks and scratchings on the shaded forest floor. Sunlight filtered down, dappling the dense moss and turning its tips crimson.

Zanna paused beside a boulder that was so overgrown with lichens it was like a miniature forest of its own. A tiny green inchworm humped its way around a patch of yellow fungus called witches'-butter. If only it had magic power. If only Zanna and Moss could eat witches'-butter to make them both invisible. Then no one would ever be able to separate them. She wished she were brave enough and smart enough to run away with him. But that would be stealing. Besides, how would she feed him?

He came crashing toward her through the branches of a fallen tree, then sat in front of her, his eyes on her face, his ears erect. She knew he was waiting for her to give him something to do. He raised one paw and placed it over her arm. This was the way she saw him sometimes with Rob. Who would ever be this close to him when she was gone?

As soon as she started home, Moss bounded ahead. She guessed that he would veer off above the house and keep on toward the sheep pasture. All right, she thought. She would follow his lead and take him to the sheep.

She tried to think of what he needed to work on. She went back over his trial run. The truth was that she was the one that needed to get her act together. It was Moss who had saved the day.

Once she and Moss were through the gate, she found herself sizing up the sheep the way she always did. In spite of her sadness, she began to plan today's practice as if it were just another session with Moss, like those that had gone before.

PART FOUR

1

Summer raced headlong toward fall. Zanna tried to slow it down. She fastened on everything around the farm—the sheep, the half-grown lambs, the calves, the crusty hen with her chicks almost feathered out.

The corn and the second hay crop faltered during the midsummer heat and then shot up quickly after a spell of rain in early August. Apples grew in Janet's orchard and also in the woods and at the edges of the fields on wild trees, hard green knobs the heifers tried to yank from low-lying branches. And down in the hollows hummocks stood as sharp reminders of the wet, cool time gone by, now dry as the mountain streambeds.

Some of Rob's old friends dropped by with news of trials and dogs. One man brought some videos. Janet came over with her VCR, and they all watched parts of the international championship trials in Scotland and a homemade collection from different trials in America. Since there wasn't time to see everything, they sampled a bit of each tape. Rob seemed to spring up like the corn after the rain. He looked as though he could have watched the videos all night.

The visitor thought Rob might enjoy seeing himself. The tape went fast forward and then slowed to show some of the handlers Zanna recognized, even Billy Mount. And yes, Rob.

Everyone fell silent as Rob on the screen strode to the post with Meg. Zanna crawled closer to the TV. So that was what Rob looked like, not very tall, solid, almost square, with a face both creased and open. And calm. Rob.

Zanna couldn't get close enough. Now the camera moved away from Rob to focus on Meg. How could anyone have guessed that viewers might crave more than this brief glimpse of Rob working his dog?

Rob's whistle sounded softer than Zanna would have expected.

At the far end of the course Meg stopped before walking on to her sheep. Then there was trouble, two of them trying to bolt. Rob's flanking whistle commands came one after the other.

There was a scrambling in the kitchen. Moss and Meg trotted into the parlor together, coming to a standstill in front of Rob. Moss glanced at the screen. At Rob's next whistle he lurched sideways.

"His master's voice," remarked the guest.

"Where are those sheep, huh?" Laurie teased Moss.

Bewildered, Moss placed himself midway between the TV and Rob and fastened him with a searching gaze.

"Aah," sighed Rob. Meg drew close to him. But Moss was caught in a kind of trance, his longing so intense and thwarted that no one there could miss it. "Aah," Rob drawled. "Aah, God!"

By now the tape was showing another handler, another dog. Everyone began to speak again. Fennella said to the visitor, "*God* means 'dog.' These days Rob can usually say it right."

But Zanna doubted that Rob was mixing up his first and last letters. She thought he had been crying out of his true grief. For how could he show the dogs that he was all that was left of the man whose whistling still called them in an instant to their feet?

The next day and the day after that Rob would not leave the house.

"The heat gets to him," Fennella declared as she sponged his face and neck. He looked to Zanna as if he were caving in on himself.

She followed Fennella out to the kitchen. Keeping her voice low, she asked whether he was staying inside because of seeing himself on tape.

Fennella beckoned her out the back door, where there was no chance of Rob's overhearing them. "That was rough, that video," Fennella answered then, "but I expect he's also pining for you and your mother. It's been a blow to him, learning you'll be so far away."

Tears filled Zanna's eyes; anger clogged her throat. She tried to choke back the words that burst from her, but she couldn't. "How can you take Moss away from him, too?"

Fennella pulled back. "Who told you?" Her tone was smooth as steel.

"I just found out. Did you think I wouldn't?"

"It may not happen." Now Fennella sounded drained. "There may not be any point to it, any need." She broke off.

Zanna understood that Fennella was referring to Rob's evaluation, about whether all the expensive changes would make any real difference. How could Zanna hope for anything less than the best outlook for Rob? Only that would mean selling Moss. "It's not fair," she mumbled.

Fennella smiled. "Never was," she agreed. "Still," she added, "look at all the good that's come out of Rob's hard time. All of you here with us. Moss coming into his power just like Rob planned. Your mom and dad getting the time they needed to work things out. A lot of good, I'd say."

Zanna turned away. She didn't want Fennella to see how sad she felt.

But Fennella noticed. And so, later, did Zanna's mother. She had timed her trip west to coincide with Rob's stay at the rehabilitation clinic. She thought Zanna might like to stay with Diane then.

Zanna's mother was startled by Zanna's fierce refusal. They both had to calm down before Zanna was able to ask whether Diane could visit her instead.

But Diane's mother would let her stay only while Zanna's mother was home, so Diane came for the last few days before Mom left. The girls split their time between playing and working at Janet and Rick's stand. Diane loved dealing with what she called the public. She was so outgoing that the customers went about their buying with broad smiles. Meanwhile, Zanna stayed as close to Janet as she could for any dog talk that might come her way.

One day, when Janet took the girls on an errand that brought them past the Coventry Fair grounds, she pointed out the race-track. Zanna craned to catch a glimpse of the grassy infield where the trial would be held. She recalled last year, her first sight of Border Collies herding sheep over a course. Had she really cared more about the midway rides and eating sugared fried dough?

While Diane was with her, Zanna didn't work Moss every morning. He let her know that he felt neglected, gazing into her eyes and slowly, hopefully, wagging his tail. Now that he had come to depend on her, they were getting closer to the time when she would have to leave him.

Diane worked at cheering Zanna up. "Your mother might find some super job out there, and then you'll be so rich you can buy him."

It was their last day together. They were sitting at the edge of the pond, which didn't smell too inviting these days and looked muddy from bottom to top. Moss and Meg swam in lazy circles. Old Queen waded in the shallows.

"Even if that happened," Zanna responded after mulling over Diane's idea, "the money would go to paying off loans." She tried to pick a black-eyed Susan, but the tough, hairy stalk wouldn't break. She ended up mauling it until the orange petals began to drop. "Anyway," she went on, "Mom wants to save for the future. For college. For Rachel," she added.

"And college for you, too, I bet."

Zanna didn't reply. A solution was forming in her head. She could trade college tuition for Moss. She mustered arguments. It would spare Mom and Dad embarrassment since she would never get into a decent college anyway. Besides, she didn't need that kind of education to be a sheep farmer.

Meg crawled out of the water and shook herself. Frogs plopped on one side and the other of her. She ignored their splashes, her eyes fixed on Moss, still swimming.

"Does he ever get tired?" Diane asked.

Zanna shook her head. That was what was wrong with her solution. Even if she could get her parents to buy Moss, he would go crazy if he had to be confined again and with no sheep to work. "He does sometimes get tired," she said, "especially when it's hot, but he never quits. He's not like other dogs."

Diane nodded. After a pause she said, "Some people have wild animals. I've seen them on television. Pet wild animals."

Zanna, her eyes on the black head showing above the pond's dark surface, knew that it wasn't the same thing. There wasn't any point saying so to Diane, who was trying so hard to figure out some angle.

"I'll never have another friend like you," Zanna said to her.

"Me, too," Diane responded. A dragonfly hovered above her drawn-up knees. Its shadow body and iridescent wings seemed suspended from an invisible thread.

Zanna reached toward it. "Sometimes they rest on you," she whispered. She brought her hand closer, closer. The dragonfly whirred and touched down for an instant before flying off to the heat-struck jewelweed, whose branches hung in limp cascades over the water.

Everything was still but for the black and white dog paddling, as if intent on some secret mission that called him on and on.

2

Mom and Fennella took Rob to the rehabilitation clinic. They left plenty of time to settle him in, so that Mom could speak to the people there and still make her flight to Chicago. Fennella had to drive home alone through a violent thunderstorm that knocked down trees and made her long, lonely trip even tougher.

At the farm the power was out, and there was trouble with the generator. When Fennella walked into the house, exhausted, Dot was down at the lower farm, helping Gordon and Dave. "We'll take care of supper, Grandma," Laurie said. "You just go crash."

"Crashing is what I've been trying to avoid for the last two and a half hours," Fennella replied. "Anyway, the sheep have to come in from the temporary electric fence. Too many coyotes around."

"Moss and I can get the sheep in," Zanna volunteered.

"Your mother wouldn't want you out in this," Fennella objected.

"It's all right," Rachel put in. "It's just raining now, that's all."

The sheep were fenced with electric netting charged by a car battery. They were in one of the lower fields that had already been hayed for a second time. The tricky bit about getting back to the home pasture was bringing them across a narrow bridge and then through the alfalfa field.

The thunder and lightning had sent Moss cowering behind the woodstove. Now, released from his terror, he charged ahead of Zanna. She could tell that he was still on the edge of panic, but the prospect of work held him in check.

The sheep were bunched at the far end of their enclosure, where maples provided shelter from the pelting rain. Zanna switched off the portable charger and then pulled back a generous length of netting. "Easy," she told Moss, who stood taut and eager. "Take time."

The sheep slid along the fence, too close. Could they tell that there was no electrical charge in it now? She worried about their getting tangled in it.

But Moss edged them away until finally he had them in the open. Then they broke and ran toward Zanna. Never before had she seen them this spooked.

She was so intent on slowing them before they reached the bridge that she flanked Moss too sharply and split the flock. "Moss!" she screamed at him. Her panic only goaded him on, driving the sheep still farther apart.

Those nearest the bridge milled about in confusion. Yelling at Moss, Zanna ran to him and slipped her fingers around his collar. The sheep that had fallen behind looked nervous, ready to bolt. She couldn't think how to fix this mess.

Then some of the forward sheep leaked away, filing across the bridge. Still clutching Moss, Zanna waited for the others in that group to follow their leaders.

Waiting was the hardest thing Moss knew how to do. When at last she sent him after the bunch that had been left behind, he made a wide outrun, despite all the trees. The sheep were so desperate to catch up with the others that Zanna had to scramble to get to the bridge first. Picking up a stick, she swung it back and forth as the sheep crashed toward her. Moss flanked without being told and kept them from scattering along the brook. Then it was just like penning. She had to keep him back to give the sheep room to march onto the bridge, just a few at a time, until they were all safely across.

After that, moving them along the edge of the alfalfa field was simple. They even snatched mouthfuls of alfalfa along the way, speeding up only as they approached the barn. Moss flanked and checked them while she sprinted to catch up. After they were safely closed in, she waited until she had stopped puffing and gasping before she and Moss, drenched and bedraggled, entered the house.

Dot and Gordon and Dave were there now. "Any trouble?" Gordon asked.

Zanna shook her head. "Everything's fine."

"Supper's ready," Dot told her. "Go change. First take a towel to that dog."

The hamburgers Laurie and Rachel had cooked over the fire were deliciously charred on the outside and slightly frozen in the middle. No one complained. The rain drummed and splashed on the house. By the flickering light of kerosene lamps everything glowed, especially the glass-fronted cabinet with Rob's trophies glinting, bearing witness to past triumphs.

Zanna gazed at them. There was nothing to show what she and Moss had just been through, the two of them blundering and then working things out. There was nothing to set on a shelf or hang on a wall. All the same she felt triumphant. Maybe Moss did, too.

The rain thinned. Thunder rumbled like an afterthought, but that was all it took to send Moss over the edge. In the kitchen there were thuds followed by frantic scratching.

"Do something about the dog," Fennella told Zanna, "before he digs through the floor."

Zanna found Moss trying to claw his way to safety as if he could bury himself beneath the dripping rain gear in the back entry. "Moss, Moss, that'll do." She spoke softly, with love.

But he was so deep in his world of danger that her voice couldn't reach him.

Three muddy boots came scudding across the kitchen floor before she was able to haul him away from the mess he had made and hug him to her.

3 One morning when Janet was at the farm to work Tess, she asked Zanna to come back with her and help out with the boys. Later she might get a chance to coach Zanna with Moss working her small flock.

They arrived at Janet's to find that Rick's mother had already taken the little ones with her for the day. So Zanna helped in the herb beds instead. Soon her fingers smelled fragrant and bitter all at the same time.

She made a discovery that day. One of the plants was called fennel. When she asked if Fennella was named for it, Janet nodded, her quick fingers packing small plants into plastic pots. Fennella's mother had grown flowers and herbs on the family island, Janet said.

Zanna thought of Rob coming out to look at the island cows and finding as well the lighthouse keeper's daughter. Now another part of the story was filled in. The lighthouse keeper's daughter was named for a plant with a distinctive sweet-sharp flavor.

"So your grandmother must have taught you about herbs," Zanna said.

Janet nodded. "And how to garden organically."

"But doesn't your father spray the corn?"

"Yes, he does. Because of the short growing season." While she spoke, Janet set the small pots of herbs in trays for customers who wanted indoor herbs for the winter. "We don't do everything alike," she went on. "I don't even train dogs exactly the way Grampa did."

"Mr. Nearing called your grandfather a living legend."

"That's the sort of thing Howard Nearing would say." Janet's lips were compressed as if she were biting off the words. She faced Zanna. "I don't want him to have Moss either. I mean, he won't harm the dog. He just won't do him any good. I wish he'd realize that he'd be a lot better off starting with a puppy of his own. I can help him with Moss, but I can't change him. Howard doesn't see that. He doesn't understand." She handed Zanna a tray of herbs. "Grampa bought Moss off a guy who was ready to shoot him. Everything had gone wrong between them. The guy blamed it all on the dog, even though Moss wasn't even a year old. So Grampa got him for practically nothing. It didn't take him long to decide that this was going to be the best dog he'd ever had. But he's not a dog for just anyone."

Zanna sighed. "I wish I'd known both of them then, Rob and Moss."

Janet squinted into the sun. Suddenly she said, "Maybe you could come east next summer and help me out here. If we still have Moss, you could work with him some more. Anyway, I'm going to breed Tess to him. I'll keep whichever puppy seems most like Moss."

Zanna's heart climbed into her throat. "What if you don't have Moss?" she managed to squeeze out.

"We'll have to see. You might be able to trial Meg."

"It's Moss—" Zanna began.

"I know," Janet said to her. "I know how you feel about him."

"My mother says it's wrong to love animals more than people."

"She's right," Janet replied. "In theory."

The truck roared up to the stand. Rachel and Laurie jumped down, followed by Rick. Soon they were all busy sorting vegetables. The wilted ones would go to Janet's house or to the farm.

Zanna worked Moss on Janet's sheep. The thought of coming back next summer buoyed her up. Janet offered pointers on handling sheep in the racetrack infield at the Coventry Fair. It would be harder to correct mistakes in that kind of space.

That night, when Mom and Dad called, Zanna tried to tell them about Janet's proposal for next summer. But they weren't ready to think that far ahead. Mom was staying out there for a second interview. She and Dad were thinking about renting a house.

"Will you be home in time for the fair?" Zanna asked her.

Dot took the phone from Zanna, saying that her parents had more pressing matters to discuss than the Coventry Fair.

The day the fair opened, Fennella set off on the long drive to bring Rob home. That evening Dave and Laurie and Rachel offered to take Zanna with them for the rides and games. Zanna was tempted. But Janet had said that since she was planning to run Meg at the trial, too, she would be up to work both Tess and Meg before dark. So Zanna stayed home to watch.

She was still waiting for Janet when Fennella pulled in with Rob. The long drive had been an ordeal for both of them. Fennella gratefully accepted Zanna's help unloading the wheelchair and getting Rob into it.

Moss stood by, waiting for a chance to sidle up close to Rob, who spoke to him quietly but lacked the energy to extend his good hand. When Zanna arranged his arm in his lap, she was struck by the dampness of his skin.

Janet arrived in time to help get Rob up the steps. While Fennella and Janet put Rob to bed, Zanna rummaged in the refrigerator and filled two plates with potato salad, ham, and pickled beets. She carried them into the back bedroom. Before Fennella could protest, Zanna said, "This is so you can keep Rob company."

Fennella glanced at Rob, who was propped against his pillows, his eyes closed. Then she heaved a sigh. Zanna went back to the kitchen to get the lemonade.

When Dot and Gordon came in from the lower farm, so did Janet, who had been out working Tess and Meg. And so did

Zanna, who had been out watching. Fennella joined everyone in the kitchen, where she reported on the results of Rob's evaluation.

His prospects were fairly good. Not that he was expected to get free of the wheelchair. But he had a good chance of becoming more self-sufficient, given the right kind of setup and equipment. She glanced briefly at Zanna, before going on to say that on the way home she had raised the matter of Howard Nearing's offer for Moss.

Gordon leaned forward. "How did Dad take it?"

Fennella sent him a long, level look before answering. "It's hard to say. I guess he's sort of resigned. I mean, a power wheelchair, changes in the house, he's not sure how much difference they'll really make. He was trying—trying to say that if they made things easier for me, for all of us . . ." Her words trailed off. "Well," she added after a moment, "he realizes the money has to come from somewhere." Her voice dropped. "I expect it's hard for him to come to terms with what he won't ever be able to do."

Dot said, her voice low, "Howard Nearing called again today. He'll be at the fair tomorrow. He was hoping we might, you know, go through with it."

Fennella shook her head. "Give Rob a little more time. He still thinks letting Moss go to Nearing is like throwing him away."

"Time!" Gordon retorted. "We could lose the deal. There's going to be a slew of good dogs at the trial. Another one could catch Nearing's eye tomorrow. Then where would we be?"

They continued to sit around the table, no one speaking. It was clear that each of them was mulling over the situation.

Finally, after a quick intake of breath, Fennella said, "I can't think anymore tonight. I'm turning in."

After she left, Dot and Gordon talked some more, not about Moss but about which changes in the house were basic necessities.

Gordon said, "We haven't any idea what will be left after we get the power wheelchair."

Janet said, "And don't forget, there's no way of knowing how long he'll be able to get along the way they say."

Gordon nodded. "We won't begrudge him, though. For whatever time he's got, we have to make it work for him."

"Grandma looks pretty beat," Janet went on. "She must have been hoping for better news."

"She'll bounce back," Dot said with confidence. "She'll feel better once she gets to be on her own with Rob. Though she needs to know that she doesn't have to manage by herself."

"We can move home gradually," Gordon suggested.

"Yes," Dot agreed. "We'll take turns, one of us staying on here till she kicks us all out."

Gordon smiled at that and launched himself out of the chair. Leaning over the sink, he sloshed water on his face and let it drip down onto his sweat-stained shirt.

Janet got up to leave. At the door she turned and spoke directly to Zanna. "You know, you've been a big part of this."

"That's true," Dot chimed in. She sent Gordon a look.

At her prompting he nodded. "Made all the difference with the dog," he told Zanna.

Zanna couldn't bring herself to say that she was glad all her work and love for Moss had paid off for them. She dropped her eyes to Moss, who had rolled over onto his back on the cool floor, with his legs in the air. He looked as though he hadn't a care in the world.

4 Cars and trucks were lined up at the livestock entrance to the fairgrounds. Tess and Meg craned to see out Janet's window. Moss leaned over Zanna's shoulder, sniffing at a trailer load of cattle. Janet had to drive all the way around the horse barns at the rear of the grounds and then up along the outside of the racetrack. She pulled in next to Beezie's pickup.

Greetings floated across the many conversations there. This was the quiet time before the competition, when everyone was hopeful and friendly. Some of the handlers were out on the course, setting up the panels to make the fetch gate, the drive gates, and the pen. One of them called to Janet to come out for a look at the chute they were making for an additional obstacle, a long, narrow corridor the dog would have to get the sheep through. Janet hitched Meg and Tess to her van and took off.

Zanna walked around with Moss. People wished her well. Someone kidded her about being in the big time now that she was running Moss in an open trial.

"It's just because there's no entry fee," Zanna tried to explain. "Janet thought it would be a good experience for both of us. But it won't be if I mess up."

"Think positive," advised a man behind her.

She whipped around, already pretty sure it was Mr. Nearing. He leaned down to stroke Moss, who wagged his tail, outgoing but impersonal.

"We're going to get along just fine," Mr. Nearing told him.

Zanna felt like informing him that this was the way Moss behaved with Rachel and Diane when they made a fuss over him. It wasn't devotion. But being rude to Mr. Nearing wasn't going to change anything.

"Rob coming today?" he asked Zanna.

"I don't know," she replied. "Fennella just brought him home last night. They were all tired out."

"I should have stopped by to see if I could help. Everyone's hoping he'll show up. I'm sure it'll do his spirits good."

Zanna didn't answer. She was thinking of how hard it was for Rob to see the video of himself and his friends. Breaking away from Mr. Nearing, she ducked between the rails and headed toward Janet.

"Don't," Mr. Nearing called to her. "Competing dogs aren't allowed on the course."

Zanna turned back, her face aflame.

"I'll hold him," Mr. Nearing offered, "if you want to go out there."

"I'll tie him up," she replied thickly, and then just managed to add, "Thanks, anyway," before leading Moss to the van.

The trial started late because the fair officials wanted to wait for an audience. The judge, a woman this time, came from England. She had been judging some trials in Canada, so she already knew many of the handlers and their dogs. She asked Zanna if she was going to run a dog today, too.

"Sort of," Zanna mumbled, suddenly aware that people were listening.

"Can't be sort of," the judge told her. "It's all or nothing."

"All," Zanna quickly replied.

"Well, good luck to you then," the judge said. She was led off to the judge's stand, which was a flatbed hay wagon positioned about midway between the starting post and the back fence. Zanna realized that the judge would be practically on top of her, with an unobstructed view of everything Moss did. She began to feel her stomach cramp up.

"Maybe I better not run Moss," she said to Janet as they looked at the order of running. More than sixty dogs were entered.

"Don't let all this get to you," Janet told her. "You're not up until after lunch. You'll get to see plenty of good runs and plenty of disasters before then. Just learn from them all."

Once during the morning Zanna took Moss for a walk around the fair. But when they neared the midway, the noise got to him. He flinched at the bells that clanged and the horns that blared and the sirens that wailed. As soon as she led him away, he relaxed enough to pick up a dusty fried onion ring that lay in his path. She stopped briefly to watch the oxen pull until she realized that Moss minded all the yelling there, too.

She got back to the trial in time to see the end of Janet's run with Meg. Although it was good, it lacked the smoothness Janet could get with Tess. The next dog to run had to be retired when it became clear that it would never complete the course. Suddenly Zanna's spirits lifted. Whatever happened with Moss couldn't possibly be that bad. He wouldn't be the worst dog of the day. That seemed to be all that mattered now: knowing that his score wouldn't be the lowest one posted.

During the lunch break word passed among the handlers that Rob had arrived. Everyone crowded around him. Mr. Nearing stood behind the wheelchair with Fennella. Zanna couldn't figure out why he was there like a member of the family. What was he doing with his hands on the wheelchair?

She took Moss down behind the horse barns and let him go for a brief run in the woods. She felt perfectly fine until she heard the announcer say her name; she was the next handler after the one just going out to the course. All of a sudden the bright day seemed to darken as if someone had set a giant lid over the sky. She could feel her heart hammering. After hurrying to the gate, she watched the run in progress in a kind of blur. She wondered if she was going to faint.

There was applause. As the handler and his dog came out from the course, Zanna walked to the post. She kept glancing up the infield at the sheep being brought out. She knew she should be thinking of which way to send Moss. Trying to focus, even fuzzily, on the sheep kept her from glancing behind her at the judge's wagon. She was simply aware of it there, looming.

Moss crouched, eyeing the sheep. Zanna needed to establish contact with him, but when she told him to stay, her voice came out cracked and wobbly. She had to whisper him away.

He shot off along the fence. He was fine. She looked ahead in time to notice that the dog holding the sheep at the top end had switched sides to keep them in position. All at once her vision cleared. She was looking where she needed to look, and here was Moss, coming around just where he ought to be. Without a word from her, he quietly started the sheep toward her. He didn't need commands when he was doing everything right.

Just before the fetch gate she flanked him left. He responded easily, and the sheep came straight through. Only as they bore down on her did they seem to press off line to her right. She tried to swing him again, to keep the fetch as good as it had begun. Only now he seemed to resist her.

"Moss!" she called sharply, to remind him of her part. His refusal to respond baffled her. He held the sheep in perfect line for a point about midway between the edge of the judge's wagon and the exhaust pen.

As the sheep slid past her and Moss failed to bring them around her to begin the first leg of the drive, she felt more surprise than anything else. Turning, she saw Rob in his wheelchair parked near the end of the wagon. What was he doing on the course? When had he been wheeled out there? How could she have missed noticing him?

Moss swung wide, bringing the sheep to a halt in front of Rob. Aghast, Zanna shouted to Moss to come bye. To her relief, he did flank to the left. Only he kept on flanking. The sheep neatly circled the man in the wheelchair. "Moss!" she shrieked. "Walk up."

But Moss simply held them in place. It was as though Rob's presence on the trial course had wiped out her own.

"Moss, Moss!" she screamed at him. She could hear the audience now, heard people talking, some of them laughing.

One sheep dodged behind the wheelchair and bolted for the exhaust pen.

"Get back out!" Zanna yelled. "Get her!"

Moss dashed after the sheep and forced her back to the cluster.

"Good boy!" Zanna called to him. "Now walk up."

When Moss stood his ground, holding the sheep in perfect order in front of Rob, the audience broke up. Over the din the announcer tried to explain what had gone wrong. But Zanna didn't listen. All she could hear was the laughter around the fence. All she could think of was getting away.

For the first time since walking onto the course, she looked up at the judge, who was speaking to the clerk, who was writing something down on Moss's score sheet. Probably the judge was telling the clerk that Moss was disqualified. Anyway, it didn't make any difference now whether Zanna stayed at the post or left it. Moss's run was finished.

Too miserable to think of what Rob must be feeling, she walked off.

When she reached the handler's gate and saw Moss's leash hanging there, she realized she couldn't leave him on the course. She grabbed the leash and turned back. Someone had already let the sheep into the exhaust pen. Someone, who might have been Mr. Nearing, was wheeling Rob out through the big gate behind the wagon.

Now that the sheep were off the course and Rob was on his way out, Moss turned expectantly to Zanna, his eye on the new group of sheep being brought out for the next dog to run. Did he think he would get another chance? Was he wondering why he hadn't been allowed to finish his run?

Zanna couldn't speak to him, couldn't utter a word of blame or comfort. All she could do was snap the leash on his collar and drag him past the incoming handler and dog. Looking neither right nor left, she kept on going until she was so far from the trial that the midway racket drowned out the announcer and the whistling that signified that another run was under way.

5

At first Zanna was scarcely aware of Moss. The midway swallowed her up. People jostled each other to seize their orders from Tish the Dough Lady. They practically trampled each other reaching for slabs of Felton's Fabulous Fritters. Those who weren't eating were shouting. And everywhere the sweet, cloying scent of spun sugar mingled with the reek of Italian sausage and bubbling fat.

Zanna, who had put off eating her sandwich until after her run, pressed past the food booths. She couldn't get rid of a bitter taste at the back of her throat. Balloons popped; plastic ducks, lined up as targets, splashed as they were hit. Some kids howled, some clutched enormous pandas or dinosaurs, while high above them the tilt-a-wheel swung its screaming riders around and around, and the Jolly Roger plunged its waving passengers into a pirate cavern.

When someone stepped on Moss's paw and he yipped and pressed against her legs, she suddenly came back to him and pushed through the mob to a quieter spot in front of a poster showing a cow with six legs and a pig with human feet. Zanna sank down on a bale of hay, which she figured was food for the animal freaks inside the tent. She drew Moss close. She knew that for him the midway clamor was a kind of punishment. She who had worried so about what his life would become had inflicted the punishment. And he couldn't know why.

Only now did she cry for herself and for him, for all she had just put him through. He pawed at her knees as if to force her up.

"There you are!" Fennella stood in front of her. "You shouldn't have the dog here. He'll be all nerved up."

Zanna wiped her sleeve across her face. "He already is. I did it to him."

"Nonsense," Fennella snapped. "You didn't do anything. It was Howard Nearing that did. Took over the wheelchair to find a good spot for Rob to see Moss run, since it's hard to see through the fence. I had no idea what he was up to, taking Rob onto the course."

"Rob let him?" Zanna exclaimed.

"Tried to stop him. But Howard wasn't listening. Rob's mad as a hornet. But he feels better now that you're getting a rerun."

A rerun? Like Billy Mount? "No way!" Zanna blurted. "I'm never going out on that course again."

Fennella leaned down to her. "Oh, yes, you are," she declared.

"No. Everyone laughed."

"Not everyone. Not those of us that understood. We kind of died for you and Rob. And for Moss. The judge could tell what happened; she saw it was outside interference on the course. Now get Moss somewhere quiet and give him a chance to unwind."

Zanna shook her head. "I can't." Her voice trembled.

"You can." Fennella sat down beside her. "Now, me"—she went on—"I couldn't. Never could. But you did, Zanna. And will. You didn't do all this work with Moss for nothing."

Moss heard his name; his tail swept the dusty ground.

"Couldn't Janet do the rerun?" Zanna asked her.

"Out of the question. You started. You finish. You can bet

Rob's counting on you to go through with it. He was kind of upset when you ran off. If you have time, after you get Moss out for a walk, you might stop by and let Rob know you don't blame him for what happened."

"I'd never blame him," Zanna exclaimed.

"How can he know that?" Fennella demanded. "You didn't say a word to him. How do you suppose he felt?"

Zanna gulped back more tears. She hadn't given Rob a thought. She had been horrible to Moss. And now it wasn't even all over.

To avoid the midway, Fennella guided them all the way around the fairgrounds, almost out to the road. They turned in at the farm machinery exhibit and crossed over at the dried flower booths. When they passed the livestock sheds, Moss began to look like himself again, glancing hopefully in the direction of the sheep and goats and cows. By the time Zanna could hear whistling from the infield of the racetrack, he seemed all restored, eager to go to work again.

Janet came to meet them, glanced at Zanna's tear-stained face, and suggested that she take Meg along for a walk with Moss. Meg would be a calming influence. Janet sounded perfectly matter-of-fact, with not a word about what had happened, only thinking ahead to the best approach for preparing Moss for his rerun. Zanna didn't think she could ever learn how to stay so cool.

After the walk Zanna hitched Meg to the van before going to look for Rob. But Mr. Nearing blocked her way. She had to stop.

"I'm sorry," he said to her. "I was sure I was doing the right thing. I ignored Rob's protests."

By now her anger and humiliation felt stale and old. She could see how crushed Mr. Nearing looked, how anxious. "It's all right," she mumbled.

"I want to make it up to you. Maybe you know that Janet will be coaching me with Moss. She says you may be back next summer. I hope to be trialing Moss by then, but I'd step aside if you wanted to run him once or twice."

Zanna nodded. She knew she ought to thank him, but all she could say was "I have to speak to Rob now."

Fennella pulled the wheelchair back when Zanna and Moss squeezed through the circle around him. That made room for them even before the people did. Moss went to rest his chin on Rob's knee. Zanna leaned over the dog and brought her smeared face close to Rob's. His eyes missed nothing.

"I lost him today," she said, her voice low. "I lost Moss."

"Some," Rob replied.

"No, completely. Lost him." And then it struck her that he was speaking in the old stroke-impaired way. *Some* was Moss.

"Zanna," he said to her, "Suzanna, don't you cry."

She knew that he wanted her to think back to the first time Moss had really worked for her when the sheep were loose on the road. She let her hands drop to either side of the motionless dog. She clutched the thick, soft coat and saw Rob's good hand descend, too, until his fingers dug through the white and black ruff and found hers.

"I won't cry," she said, rising. "I have to run Moss again. He gets weird when I cry."

6 It had been a long day, and the sheep were getting resistant. Zanna had to absorb everyone's last-minute tips. Apparently it was only an advantage to run last if the sheep hadn't been run too many times already.

Zanna wasn't especially nervous, though. The worst had happened. She watched the sheep try to break from the dog that held them at the top end of the infield. When it was clear that they weren't going to settle, the judge told her to send her dog anyway.

Moss never had a chance to complete his outrun. The sheep came barreling down the course. Now what? No one had given her any advice about what to do in a situation like this. She wheeled around to the judge.

"Watch your dog," the judge told her. "Watch your sheep."

Moss was just as thrown as she was. He stood partway up the course, waiting for a command. All right, thought Zanna. She had just lost all his outrun and lift points. All she could do was rescue what was left of the fetch and then go on with the drive.

She had to swing Moss wide to keep the sheep from charging toward the exhaust gate. As soon as he brought them around behind her, they slowed. Now she could collect her thoughts. She would have to keep Moss from pressing the sheep too hard.

He fell in on a right flank, quietly keeping pace with the sheep and holding them on a straight line for the first drive gates. She knew she must turn the sheep as soon as they came through, so that they wouldn't take off for the top end of the infield.

She sent Moss wide to the left. He shot around, almost too close. But after that he marched the sheep straight across to the second gates. As they trotted through, Moss managed to scoop them away from the fence, which was just ahead of them. Now she was allowed to leave the handler's post and go to the chute. It was like maneuvering the Catherwood sheep across the bridge, except that she couldn't pick up a stick to use as a crook. When she waved her arms instead, that rattled the sheep. So she held still and brought Moss to a full stop while the sheep drifted across the mouth of the chute. Then she shifted her own position a bit and whispered to Moss to come bye. That was all it took. The lead sheep turned and led the others into the narrow opening.

Zanna ran to the pen. Without being commanded, Moss kept the sheep moving quietly toward her. They walked right in, as if they realized they were coming to the end of their run.

What remained was the shed, something Zanna and Moss had

never practiced together. She brought the sheep into the shedding ring, figuring that Moss could just keep them there until the time ran out. But when they lined up in one direction, she couldn't resist trying to single off the last sheep.

"Moss!" Zanna shouted. "Here, Moss!"

He sprang forward, just in front of the one to be shed from the others. For a long moment it simply faced him. Then it gave in, turning away from the dog's intense stare, and trotted out of the ring.

The applause was tremendous, even though most of the audience had moved on to the midway or had gone home for dinner. But the diehard sheepdog enthusiasts and all the handlers remained to cheer Moss and Zanna as they came out of the infield.

Fennella pushed Rob toward her. She let Moss go to him. Only then did she realize how wonderful she felt.

Everyone was in a hurry to get going. Many of the handlers had hours of driving ahead. Everybody was talking about some deal or other that had been organized during the day. They decided to put off an emergency meeting that had been called, so that everyone could get under way as soon as possible. They could take care of the matter later on.

The trial manager thanked the judge and all the handlers. He also said that a special presentation planned for this time had been postponed. Then he explained that there were money awards for fifteen places and ribbons for ten.

It didn't matter to Zanna that Moss couldn't hope to place because of his botched outrun. She wasn't even curious about his score. She already knew that Janet had placed Tess in the top ten.

The manager began with the dog that had placed fifteenth. He gave the handler an envelope. Fourteenth went to Beezie's dog. Zanna clapped with all her might. "And thirteenth," he announced, "goes to Rob Catherwood's Moss run by Zanna Wald."

Zanna was stunned. She didn't step forward to receive her envelope. She just shook her head and tried to explain that there had been a mistake, that Moss had no points for his outrun and lift. The judge had to tell her that when a dog gets a rerun, the scoring starts from where the interference occurred.

"Your points for the outrun, lift, and most of the fetch were earned during your first run," said the judge, "before Mr. Catherwood got in the way."

Everyone laughed.

Zanna blurted, "But is that fair?"

"It's the rule," the judge replied.

"Oh," said Zanna as the manager handed her the envelope.

"I'm sorry there's no ribbon," he said to her.

"That's all right," she answered. "We have one at home."

She was included in the group that extended and received congratulations. Then Janet asked her to hitch Moss to the van and come help dismantle the course. The handlers who didn't have far to travel usually helped at the end of the trial.

But Mr. Nearing was waiting for Zanna. Once again he stopped her. "That was splendid," he said. "Rob must be very proud."

She couldn't hold back a smile.

"I meant what I said before," he went on. "I put you through a lot. I think I have an idea you might like." He paused.

She said, "I'm supposed to help take down the course."

"My idea is that you could become part owner of Moss. It would just be symbolic, of course. Still, if you want that, there's a way."

Zanna shook her head. "How?"

"Buy a percentage of him."

Zanna didn't understand. She said, "I can't buy anything. I don't have any money."

He nodded at the envelope she was holding. "What's in there?"

She hadn't thought to look. Now she opened the envelope and counted out four ten-dollar bills. She showed them to him.

"Unless you have other plans for the money," he said, "that could buy you one percent of this dog."

How could she have plans? She had never expected to win anything. "Maybe it belongs to Rob, though," she said.

Mr. Nearing smiled. "I doubt he'd see it that way. You earned it, you and Moss. If you want, you can take it home to show your family. You can always give it to me later. Or keep part of it. Or all of it. I don't need your money, Zanna. I'm just trying to help."

She nodded. It didn't take her long to reach a decision. "All of it," she said. "So that Moss will always be partly mine."

"Fine," he said. "Do you want to tell Rob about it?"

That must mean that Rob had finally agreed to let Moss go to Mr. Nearing. She wondered when that had happened. "I want to give the money to Rob," she said. "Is that all right? Will Moss still be partly mine?"

"Certainly," Mr. Nearing assured her. "It's still part of the price."

Fennella had Rob beside the truck, with many more helpers than she could use to get him and the wheelchair loaded. He looked worn-out, but his face was creased with smiling.

Dropping down beside him, Zanna said that she would like to buy in on Moss with all forty dollars from today's win. Was that all right? Did Rob think it was hers to spend that way?"

Rob nodded. "Zanna's," he said. "Yes."

"No receipt?" Fennella asked.

"What's that?" Zanna responded.

"Proof of payment," Fennella explained.

Everyone began to laugh. Flustered, Zanna asked why Rob

needed proof if he had the money. That just made everyone laugh harder.

Zanna looked at Rob, who was laughing, too, in that drawling way that still sounded like the echo of a sob. If he could laugh, even at her, then it had to be all right. No need to take offense and run off to the midway.

Rob thrust himself forward to free his good hand. Zanna saw it creep to his knee and then stop with the fingers extended toward her.

"Well," Mr. Nearing declared, "it looks like Rob wants to shake on it before you change your mind."

Zanna took Rob's hand in both of hers until she could fit his clasp in a proper handshake with her.

"That clinches it," Fennella declared. "And now it's time to go home."

7

The last few days on Ragged Mountain were full of frenzied packing and endless discussions about arrangements for a future in which Zanna had no part. Her mother was busy at the hospital and even busier at home.

Rachel begged to be allowed to go to school when it started, even though she would be gone at the end of the following week. So Mom gave in. Anything for peace, she told the girls. That meant Zanna could go, too, if she wanted to.

But Zanna had no intention of spending these last precious days away from Moss, who was not to be let go until after she left. She kept more or less to the summer routine, helping Janet out with the little boys, visiting with Rob, moving portable fence with Fennella, and talking on the telephone with Diane.

Most of all, though, she just hung out with Moss. She worked him first thing every morning and then again whenever Janet was available.

One day Zanna and Fennella got Rob out the back way and over to the sheep pasture gate. Rob struggled to give Zanna pointers. It was hard. First she had to figure out which phase of work he was talking about. Then she had to recall it well enough to apply his correction to it.

Afterward Moss went tearing down to the pond to cool off, returning to sit between them, while Rob pronounced and mispronounced the crucial words and Zanna groped to make sense of them. Each time Rob clapped his good hand on his knee, Zanna guessed that she'd got it right. Then she repeated what he wanted her to learn or try. Their mutual delight stirred Moss to thrust his wet muzzle first at one of them and then the other, binding them with his love.

Now that the nights were growing cool, Zanna was able to get Moss on her bed at least for a while. But any foot movement under the covers still spooked him. She would lie as still as she could bear to be, but the moment she rolled over or even shifted her position, he gave his nervous growl and bounded off the bed. Then, in a matter of moments, he leaped back up again.

Each time he returned to her that way, she spoke to him about coming back. Maybe some understanding would linger with him after he went to live with Mr. Nearing.

"I'm coming back," she told him. "Going away and coming back. So are you. We'll both come back to Janet's."

Moss would gaze at her, his dark eyes fastened on her face. He would prod her with one black-spotted white paw. Then he would groan and stretch out, laying claim to his place beside her. Until the next time she moved.

On their long walks she kept up the language of their coming separation. She would be striding along, with Moss far ahead, when something would stop her in her tracks—the blazing leaves of a swamp maple already turned scarlet, or a pair of broad-winged hawks banking down the sky, or the russet flash of a fox vanishing among the tumbled stones of an old wall. When Moss, way beyond her, suddenly realized she wasn't following, he would circle back to check on her.

"You went away," she would tell him. "You came back."

She would see him tense at the magic word, *away*, in case she meant to send him away to me, casting him out in a great circle that always ended in return.

"I'm coming back," she promised him. "Coming back, like you."

Moss would respond with a look imploring her to keep up with him. Then he would set off again, easy in his freedom and confident that she would never let him get too far away from her.

When the moving van came early on the second to last day, Zanna made the mistake of hanging around the house. Moss lurched from one haven to another. But no place was safe for long. In his terror of a menacing bureau, he would blunder into the path of a tilted bookcase or bed.

So Zanna took him up to her room, almost Laurie's room now, where the furniture stood still.

As soon as the movers finished their loading, Mom went over to the farm to work with Rob, whose morning therapy she had missed. Zanna went back upstairs to check on Moss, who had taken over the bed and was lying full length, recovering from the morning's ordeal. She loved seeing him this way, as if he had taken possession of this space and knew that this was where he belonged. She stroked the white blaze that always looked so clean above his speckled muzzle.

She was trying to decide whether to take him for a walk or work the sheep when Mom turned up with a surprising announcement. "You're invited to the farm for lunch."

That sounded strange. Zanna was never invited to lunch.

Either she was there at lunchtime and was included at the table, or else she wasn't.

"Zanna, did you hear me?" Mom called up to her.

Zanna came out to the landing. "Why?"

Mom looked harried. "They're having trouble with Rob. He won't sign some papers. Fennella's upset. Gordon's having a fit. They need you to help straighten things out."

Zanna had an awful feeling that this had something to do with Moss. "Is Mr. Nearing there?" she asked suspiciously.

Mom looked startled. "No."

"Why can't you help?" Zanna demanded.

"I tried. We even got Janet to come over. And," she added, "Janet was as reluctant as we guessed you'd be. But at least she tried."

This felt to Zanna like some kind of trap. "Rob always listens to Janet," she said.

"Not this time. Rob's refusing to sign Moss over to Mr. Nearing, to transfer the registration. Gordon's afraid he's backing down."

Zanna leaned over the stair rail. "Rob refuses?" She tried to keep her voice level. Inside, she shook with elation and hope.

"I said I'd bring you over. No one wanted to put you through this, but they don't have any choice. Rob maintains that he's already sold Moss. To you."

Zanna called Moss from his perch on the bed. She told herself that after all nothing was changed. She was just going to the farm to say what everyone already knew. All Rob had sold her was one percent of Moss. To make her feel better. The Catherwood family needed her to clear up Rob's confusion, that was all.

8   When Zanna and Mom arrived at the farm, all the
    Catherwoods except Dave and Laurie were gath-
ered in the kitchen. Lunch was on the table. Rob was pulled up
to it, a form of some kind spread out in front of him.

"Leave Moss outside," Gordon said curtly.

"What difference does it make," snapped Fennella, "whether
he's in or out?"

"Adds to the confusion," Gordon muttered.

They made room for Zanna, who sat down across from Rob.
The others stood.

"Now," said Gordon, "we're going to go through this one
more time. Dad, last Saturday morning, before you went to the
fair, you agreed to sell Moss to Howard Nearing."

"Ungreed," Rob answered.

"You agreed," Gordon insisted.

Fennella said, "Gordon, don't raise your voice to your father."

Gordon drew a long breath and started over. "You made us
promise certain things. Janet was to have input. Howard had to
promise you or Janet first refusal if he decided to unload the dog.
Janet can back me up. Right?"

He turned his gaze on Janet, who echoed dully, "Right."

Fennella said, "You never mentioned changing your mind,
Rob. Did it happen when Zanna paid you at the fair?"

Rob nodded. "Done," he said in a clear, firm voice.

Zanna felt someone nudge her between the shoulders. "Speak
up," Dot told her. "He needs to hear from you what you paid
for."

"It was just forty dollars." The words came out a whisper.

"He needs to hear you loud and clear," Dot prompted from
behind her.

"I only gave you forty dollars," Zanna shouted. She stared down at the plate of beans someone had set in front of her. She had managed not to cry, but she wasn't at all sure she wouldn't throw up.

"Now, Dad, how about signing the transfer of registration so we can all get on with lunch and go back to work?" Gordon placed a pen in Rob's good hand and slid the form closer to him. "We can fill in the name," he said. "You just sign it."

Janet walked to the door.

"Aren't you staying?" Dot asked her.

"No way," said Janet, sounding sad and angry all at the same time. "This isn't working because it's no good. Don't you see that? Grampa does."

"Your grandfather's going to sign now," Dot informed her. Zanna's mother straightened the pen he gripped and positioned the registration certificate for him.

Janet strode out to the porch, where Zanna could see her through the window as she stooped down for a moment. Zanna guessed Janet was having a word with Moss.

Everyone in the kitchen watched Rob labor to put the name on the transfer line.

"Wait," said Mom, who stood behind him. "Rob, all they need is your signature. Someone else can fill in—" She broke off, casting a glance at Fennella. Then she shook her head.

"What?" demanded Gordon. "What did he do?" He walked around for a look, then groaned.

Dot joined him. "It's all right," she said. "You can write over it. It isn't even a name."

"What isn't a name?" asked Fennella. "Rob can sign perfectly well now."

Zanna's mom pushed the registration certificate toward Fennella and said, "I'm afraid he's transferred ownership to the wrong person."

"Not wrong," Rob declared.

"Oh, Rob," Fennella said to him. Zanna thought she sounded sad but not angry.

"Maybe it's not what it looks like," Dot suggested. "It doesn't spell Suzanna, and there's no last name. It can be fixed."

"No," Fennella declared. "It's done. It's Rob's decision."

"You're giving in?" Dot exclaimed.

"Well, I'm not going to bully him. I've never been able to, and I'm not about to try now. Rob knows his own mind."

"But he doesn't understand what's at stake," Gordon objected.

Fennella rested her bony elbows on the table beside Rob. "Do you?" she asked. "And do you understand that Zanna paid you only one percent of what Howard Nearing intended to pay for Moss?"

"Zanna," Rob answered. "Paid. All she has."

"There goes the power wheelchair," Gordon remarked. "Do you understand that, too, Dad?"

"But he's getting a wheelchair!" Mom blurted. "Hasn't anyone told you yet?"

All the Catherwoods except Rob turned to her, while she explained what she knew. "They took a collection at the fair. All the sheepdog handlers. Then they were worried that they didn't have enough, so they rounded up some more donations. First they were going to give Rob a check. Then they decided to present him with the chair. The fair kicked in with the balance."

"How did you find all this out?" Fennella demanded.

"They started calling me as soon as I got home from California. They wanted my advice on the right kind of chair. A friend of Janet's is handling it."

"Beezie," said Zanna, so dazed that she could only focus on this one detail.

"Right," said Mom. "Did you know about it, too?"

Zanna shook her head. "That's Janet's friend. I didn't know

anything about what was going on that day. I don't even know
what's happening now."

Fennella picked up the registration certificate, shoved Zanna's
untouched plate aside, and set the paper in front of her. Zanna
stared at Moss's pedigree, lines and lines of names and numbers.
Her eye finally fell to the bottom, where a scrawled signature
took off from the space it was supposed to fill. Beside it, more
of Rob's handwriting spilled over beyond the transfer line. Zanna
made out letters that seemed to spell *Szana*. She looked up at
Mom.

"We can't possibly—" Mom began to protest.

"Janet can," Rob replied. "Moss keep Janet."

It began to sink in. Moss would stay here with Janet. He was
safe.

"We'll have to rethink all the plumbing," Gordon pointed out.

"There'll be more puppies coming along," Fennella reminded
him. "That's always like found money."

Gordon pulled back a chair and sank into it. "Who gets to
break the news to Howard Nearing?" he asked.

No one spoke.

"Poor man," Fennella finally said. "He tried so hard."

"Mr. Nearing had quite a lot to do with the wheelchair fund,"
Mom put in.

"Great," muttered Gordon. "Rub in the guilt."

"Give him pick of the litter out of Tess and Moss," Dot suggested.

"Janet's planning to keep a Moss pup," Zanna informed her.

Dot heaved a sigh. "So tell him he gets second pick. *And* Janet
will help him train it."

Gordon said, "I'd better clear that with Janet before I make
any more deals with Howard Nearing."

Zanna said, "And will you tell him for me that if Janet thinks
it's all right, he can trial Moss once or twice next season?"

"Are you sure?" Fennella asked. "You only just got the dog."

Zanna nodded. She couldn't begin to explain how she felt. Moss had been hers almost as long as she had known him, Rob's and hers both. She said to Fennella, "That was what Mr. Nearing was going to let me do. So it's fair. Only it has to be up to Janet."

"Want to tell him yourself?" asked Gordon as he helped himself to cold beans and brown bread. "You're the winner here."

Rob spoke up across from her. "No. Moss winner."

Zanna sent him a grateful smile, which he answered with his lopsided grin.

She turned to Fennella. "Can I go now? Is it all right?" Moss was waiting for her on the porch. She wanted to go somewhere alone with him. Maybe back to the field where they had first walked together and apart. At last she felt ready to face that memory. And Moss? Could he remember it, too?

Fennella nodded. "You and Rob better finish the paperwork first."

Zanna took the certificate to Rob. She tried to fit the pen in his hand the way her mother had. Then she placed her own hand over Rob's to help him steady his writing. She saw her last name appear on the line where it belonged. But Rob wasn't finished. Slowly, deliberately, he added the farm address, imperfectly spelled, but clear to anyone who cared to understand.

GLOSSARY

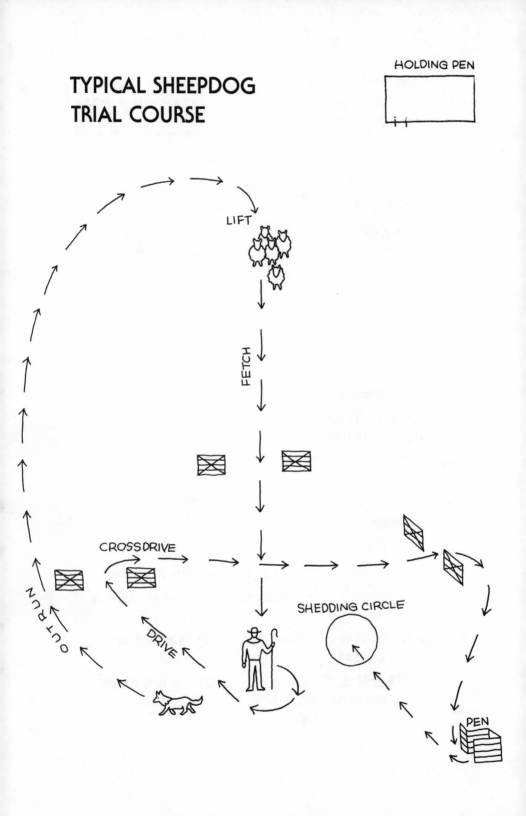

Sheepdog trial—Herding competition.

Outrun—Dog is sent left or right all the way out and around sheep, which may be as far as five hundred yards from handler.

Lift—Dog takes control of sheep.

Fetch—Dog brings sheep straight to handler and around behind handler.

Drive—Dog drives sheep away through first drive gates and across course through second drive gates and then to shedding ring or pen.

Pen—Handler leaves post to assist dog, which pens sheep, then brings them out of pen to shedding ring.

Shed—Within marked circle dog cuts off one or more sheep from group and forces them away.

Holding pen—Place where sheep are kept, a few used for each competing dog.

Exhaust pen—Place where sheep are put away after dog completes its run.

Flank—The dog keeps to one side of the sheep to move them in a straight line.

Head—The dog goes beyond flanking position to slow or turn sheep.

Flocking—The instinctive clustering of sheep for security.

Eyeing—The Border Collie stare that controls the sheep.

"Away to me"—The command for the dog to go right or counterclockwise.

"Come bye"—The command for the dog to go left or clockwise.

"That'll do"—The command for the dog to leave the sheep and return to handler.

EXHAUST PEN